HER VIKING WOLF

50 LOVING STATES, COLORADO

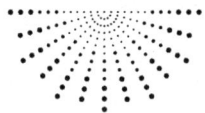

THEODORA TAYLOR

HER VIKING WOLF

by Theodora Taylor

Copyright © 2013 by Theodora Taylor

First E-book Publication: March 2013

Free Book Alert!!!

Want a FREE Theodora Taylor Book?

Join Theodora's mailing list to get a free welcome book along with newsletter-only exclusive stories, author giveaways, and special sales.

Go to theodorataylor.com for your FREE BOOK

All rights reserved.

No part of this book may be reproduced in any form or by any electronic or mechanical means, including information storage and retrieval systems, without written permission from the author, except for the use of brief quotations in a book review.

HER VIKING WOLF

Sexy Time-traveling Viking Shifter Alert!

When Chloe Adams was four, her shiftless shifter parents abandoned her on the side of the road. But now she's reinvented herself as a DIY domestic goddess, and she's engaged to the most eligible alpha in Colorado –- that is until a huge, red haired, time-traveling Viking werewolf shows up to claim her as his fated mate.

Wait... what?!?!

READER WARNING: This smoking-hot romance contains jaw-dropping twists and turns, sizzling sex scenes, and nothing less than the adventure of a lifetime. HER VIKING WOLF went on to become an instant fan favorite, but should only be read by those who like their Vikings red-haired and red-hot!

And don't forget to check out the other books in the Alpha series!

ALPHA KINGS
Her Viking Wolf
Wolf and Punishment
Wolf and Prejudice
Wolf and Soul
Her Viking Wolves

ALPHA FUTURE
Her Dragon Everlasting
NAGO: Her Forever Wolf
KNUD: Her Big Bad Wolf
RAFES: Her Fated Wolf
Her Dragon Captor
Her Dragon King
Get them all at theodorataylor.com

CHAPTER ONE

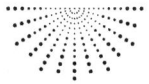

"SO have you thought about what you're going to wear on your first heat night?" Rafe asked Chloe as they climbed up King's Trail, their boots crunching in the freshly driven snow.

Despite the frigid mountain air, Chloe's cheeks went hot with embarrassment. "No," she answered, keeping her voice as neutral as possible, so as not to betray how uncomfortable this subject made her. "Have you?"

Rafe slid her the most wicked of grins. "I'm thinking red lace, maybe some of those black garters. If you give me your measurements, I can put in an order online and have exactly what I want to see you in sent over to your place."

At that moment, Chloe was grateful for the darkness of her skin, because she could feel her initial blush spreading over her entire body. And this despite the fact she was wearing little more than her favorite hand-knitted sweater over one of the many long prairie dresses she'd also made herself and favored even when she wasn't filming episodes of Black Mountain Woman. Why did having these kinds of conversations with Rafe always make her so uneasy? He wasn't just her fiancé, he was also her best friend—really her only truly close friend offline—and she'd become accustomed to bringing all of her problems to him.

But of course, she couldn't tell him how uncomfortable it made her to talk with him about anything of a sexual nature. Was this how all she-wolves who hadn't gone into heat felt about the subject of sex? If she were a normal person, she would go to the internet with her problem. Find a forum of similar women with a similar issue. Or maybe she'd consult one of her Black Mountain Woman fans. Many of them had come to feel like real friends over the three years she'd hosted her blog and YouTube show, and she knew at least a few of them had navigated their way around sticky relationship issues.

However, the North American Lupine Council had strictly forbidden talking on the internet about anything involving their species. It was bad enough, in their opinion, that interest in werewolves was at an all time high these days, with everything from books to movies being made about their supposedly mythical race. Better not to fuel the frenzy with a blog or forum that any non-paranormal could happen across.

Besides, even if she were able to reach out to other she-wolves on line, she doubted she would find much commiseration. There were only a few hundred alpha wolves in the entire world, and Rafe Nightwolf, the alpha prince of Colorado, had chosen her, a nobody she-wolf who had literally been abandoned at the side of the road outside their shifter town.

Rafe also happened to be ridiculously hot, with his Native American father's high cheekbones and long, sharp nose, softened by the light brown eyes and toasted brown skin he'd inherited from his Latina mother. When he'd proposed to her in front of everyone at their high school graduation, the other young she-wolves in their class had only been half-joking about how jealous they were. Any other she-wolf would kill to have a werewolf as good-looking and well off as Rafe ask for her hand in marriage.

He was also kind and had proven himself to be incredibly

patient. So far he'd waited over six years to consummate their relationship, since North American Lupine Council law forbade marrying or even mating with a she-wolf who hadn't yet had her first heat. Most she-wolves went into heat between the ages of sixteen and twenty-one, which was why female wolves tended to marry and start their families rather young by modern standards.

However, Chloe had turned twenty-five a couple of months ago, and even Rafe's seemingly infinite patience was showing signs of wearing thin. He'd been snapping at her more and more lately for little things like wearing her prairie dresses to formal events and spending too much time working on her Black Mountain Woman shows. He'd also begun bringing up their heat night whenever they were alone together, imagining out loud what they would do and how they would do it. And though she'd had six years to get used to the idea, and had even watched a few porn movies in the hopes it would jump start her into heat, she still couldn't bring herself to talk about it or even fully imagine it in her own head.

"Hey, did I tell you? I'm working on a chicken and fennel recipe for the next episode of *Black Mountain Woman*," she said, covering up her rather unsubtle subject change with a bright smile. "Maybe I'll have it ready in time for the wedding."

He gave her a quizzical look, "You're marrying an alpha prince. You can't cook for your own wedding."

"Why not?"

"What would people say?" he asked. "Listen, Clo, you know I love you and I support your weird hobby as much as I can, but I've got to draw the line somewhere. We'll have people flying in from all over the world to attend our wedding. You can't serve them homemade chicken and fennel."

Chloe opened her mouth to argue. First of all, he didn't really support her *Black Mountain Woman* projects. She'd garnered hundreds of thousands of fans over the years with her from-scratch recipes, DIY crafting projects, and organic cleaning tips. She was also able to support herself off the money she made from advertisers on her blog and her YouTube revenue stream. But her own fiancé referred to what she did for a living as a "weird hobby." One, she knew without having to discuss it, he expected her to give up as soon as they married.

But before she could point out any of this, he asked, "Why is it every time I bring up our heat night, you change the subject to *Black Mountain Woman?*"

"Um…" She scrambled to come up with a good excuse, but could only produce a weak, "Do I?"

He regarded her with cool eyes. "Yeah, you do."

Silence descended as they continued to press up the mountain. Many of her fellow wolves loved to hike King's Trail, but Chloe had never seen the appeal of walking up a steep precipice just because. Her glutes were already starting to protest this rare trip to the portal, a gate through space and time, which was located on a plateau about two miles up the mountain that bordered Wolf Springs. According to their lookout, Jeb, who had a cabin nearby, it flashed thirty minutes ago, which meant they had a visitor. Maybe even one from the past.

Alpha princes acted in a somewhat vice presidential role for their pack until they inherited the throne, and though she hated making the somewhat arduous trip to the portal, greeting the werewolves who had come through it had been one of her favorite duties so far as Rafe's future wife.

Technically wolves used the portal for one of two reasons. The first was to punish wolves, who had committed acts so heinous they were banished, not only from their communities but also from their own space and time. However, the last recorded instance of that happening had been when Rafe's own mother, Lacey, was the future alpha princess. Lacey still occasionally told the story of how a werewolf had come through the gate, still-shifted and frothing white at the mouth. The crazed thing had leapt at her and Rafe's dad barely had time to pull his gun and put a silver bullet in its head before it got to her.

To this day, the king still made them carry tranquilizer guns when they made these trips, even though a banished wolf hadn't come through the gate in almost three decades. No, these days, most of their visitors were using the gate for its second intended purpose: to find one's fated mate.

Fated mates spells had fallen out of fashion in modern times, and most had been lost to the winds of history. But about once a year a she-wolf from another place and/or time, came through the portal. These she-wolves were usually at two ends of a rather extreme spectrum: silly romantics, who hadn't fully considered the repercussions of a spell that could literally rip them out of their current space and time, or women who were well-ahead of their time or couldn't fit in with their own societies. They'd had a pre-Civil War southern debutante come through the gate the year before, but prior to that, they'd gotten one suffragette and one modern she-wolf from a middle-eastern country that put serious restrictions on women's rights.

She glanced at the tranquilizer gun, which she kept hidden in a vintage leather holster at her hip, and wished she could just get rid of it altogether. Holsters and prairie dresses didn't really go together.

"Who do you think it will be?" she asked, when they were about five minutes away from the gate. She was once again changing the subject, but she hoped he wouldn't call her on it this time.

Rafe shrugged. "You never know."

That was when they heard a groan.

"Did you hear that?" Chloe asked, dropping her voice and wishing she'd brought a first aid kit. "Do you think she was hurt? The portal spits people out so hard."

"No," Rafe pulled out his tranq gun. "It sounded male."

They carefully approached the portal, an invisible rift in space and time that a lycanthrope could feel but couldn't quite see, unless it was sucking a wolf in or spitting one out. And indeed, they soon spotted a large figure passed out in the snow and facing away from them.

Definitely male, Chloe thought. The top half of his torso was uncovered, revealing a back that was hard with muscle, even in repose. A pair of leather pants covered his legs, which were as thick as tree trunks, and probably just as hard if they matched his back. No, even though long, red hair fell to his shoulders in thick, tangled waves, Chloe could sense his maleness from his smell alone, an intense mix of wood, animal blood, and testosterone.

"Stay behind me," Rafe told her. He edged closer to the semi-unconscious shifter and used one booted foot to turn him over.

Chloe did as she was told but even from behind Rafe, she could see the man had a hard and serious face, half of which was covered with a thick, red beard. His hand was clutched tightly around a sword, which featured an ivory grip, a large iron wolf at the top of its hilt, and a double-edged steel blade. It was coated in blood, and looked wickedly sharp. Luckily the werewolf, who had been on the verge of unconsciousness when he groaned earlier, seemed to be completely unconscious now.

She spotted a large rock near where his head now lie. "He must have hit his head on that rock when he came out of the portal. Maybe we should move it. I'd hate for the next person who came through to get hurt, especially if it's a she-wolf."

"Check the gnarly beard on this guy," Rafe said, lowering his gun. "He looks like a Viking, right?"

Chloe stepped from behind Rafe to fully observe the unconscious man. "He's either a Viking or a very strange rock star, and I've never seen a rock star with—"

Suddenly the maybe-Viking's eyes popped open. And that was all the warning they got before he yanked on Rafe's leg, pulling him to the ground and jumping to his own feet. As Rafe's tranq gun went flying across the snow, the red-haired man pinned Rafe with a large bare foot planted squarely in the middle of his chest. And his eyes blazed with a warrior's fury as he raised his vicious-looking sword above his head with the blade pointed downward. Chloe didn't know a lot about sword fighting, but even she could tell this was the preparation for a killing blow.

"No!" she screamed, raising her own tranq gun and pointing it at the mad wolf.

He paused and looked toward her, pinning her with a piercing gray gaze that looked like it had been fashioned from the same material as his steel sword.

Chloe just hoped to the heavens above that whatever time period this wolf was from, he understood what a gun was—even if hers technically wasn't a real one.

"Put the sword down or I'll shoot," she said, hating that she couldn't keep her voice from trembling as she issued this command.

She half-expected him to kill Rafe then come after her. He'd pinned Rafe so quickly, he'd probably be able to do away with them both before she managed to squeeze the trigger. But he didn't kill Rafe or her. He just stood there staring, his eyes flinty under the midday sun.

Several seconds ticked by, but he did not look away.

And eventually he said something to her in a thick, coarse language that sounded a little like German, but she couldn't be sure. Oh God, he probably really was a Viking, she realized.

"Um," she said, wishing now that she hadn't chosen to take three years of high school Spanish as opposed to a language that might actually be useful when dealing with a possible Viking werewolf. Her mind fumbled around for any German she knew, and started spewing every single word and phrase, in the hopes something would stick. "*Dankeshein?* Um...*neinn*...*sprechen sie Englisch?* Um...um, oh my God, *Auf Wiendersehn?*"

He squinted at her. Then to her great alarm, he lowered the sword and came stalking straight toward her.

"Um, stop. Stop, please! Stay right where you are!" How did you say "stop" in German? She had no idea.

In the end, she squeaked, squeezing the trigger, and her eyes shut at the same time.

She heard a hard thump and when she opened her eyes, the maybe-Viking was lying crumpled on the ground with a dart lodged in his shoulder, already rendered unconscious by the fast-acting sleep agent it administered.

Beyond him, she could see Rafe, now sitting up and shaking his head. "Chloe…"

She re-harnessed her tranquilizer gun. "I know, I know, tranq the wolf first, ask questions later."

"Especially when he has a sword pointed at my freaking neck." Her normally indulgent fiancé didn't look too happy with the Viking or her at that moment. "And do I really need to tell you not to close your eyes when you shoot?"

CHAPTER TWO

MANY CENTURIES AGO...

"FENRIS, I would have words with you," his aunt, Bera, said. The small woman did not wait for his assent before falling in step beside him, and he had to switch his bloodied sword to his other hand to keep from staining her clothes with it.

Even his respect for his aunt's advanced years could not keep the terseness he felt out of his voice when he answered, "Whatever it is can wait until I have washed in the lake. I am fresh from the hunt."

With pursed lips, she pressed a linen rag, with words written across it in charcoal ink, into his hand.

"What is this?" he asked, though he had a feeling he already knew. His lack of a mate was a subject well-visited by his aunt, even more so since he had reached twenty and seven winters.

"I have bid you too many times to seek your fated mate. You have not heeded me, mayhap because I am but a decrepit she-wolf. Thusly, I have put the spell down for you on this scrap, in the hopes you would bestow joy upon my heart by speaking it as I have written it."

He looked from the spell to his aunt who despite her gray hair, much smaller size, and supposed decrepitude managed to keep up with his fast pace. "You realize I will disappear if I speak these words on my tongue?"

"I have put to words the return spell on the reverse side of the rag. You and your fated mate have only to speak them as one and you will be returned to this place."

He held the rag out to his aunt. "You are dear to me, sister of my father, but you try my patience with this business. I will claim a mate of my own accord. I do not wish to be fated."

His aunt clenched her hands by her side, refusing to take the linen back from him. "Your sires were fated."

"Yes, and this be the reason I wish not to be," he answered.

"Your mother and father were very happy before…"

She did not finish, but she did not have to. Fenris knew the rest. His sires were very happy, until his mother died giving birth to him, before his father was reduced to a husk of his former self in his grief.

"I do not wish a fated mate," he repeated. "Take this back. I have no use for it."

A knowing smile played on his aunt's lips. "We shall see. This winter has been cold and dark. You will eventually want for a mate to warm your bed. Why not put yourself in the hands of the gods?"

His aunt was the last person he wanted to talk to on this subject, even if she was correct about the state of his bed. He had not lain with a woman since his visit to the human market to the south of them before the last summer moon. There, he and his unmated pack members could lie with human women willing to trade their services for the furs, iron, small weapons, and the other items his village was known to sell.

"Aunt Bera, the only thing I want for now is my soap."

She stopped walking. "And you may have it. I will take my leave, but will leave you with the spell." She then turned and hurried back toward their village before he could offer any further protest.

He balled the fabric up inside his hand. Having stripped down to bare feet and his leather hunting trousers in preparation for his bath, he had nothing with which to pin it to his clothing. However, he also did not want to leave it lying around for any young she-wolf to find. She-wolves could be silly when it came to matters of the heart, and even though most of them had no knowing of written words, they might seek someone who did to help them speak the words. In the past, his aunt had taken great care not to record the spell for fear it would fall into the wrong hands.

That she had written the spell down for Fenris without his having asked it, proclaimed her frustration with his refusal to take a bride more loudly than any words ever could. But he did not want to dwell on her actions. He was fresh from the hunt, having taken down no less than three reindeer and a bear, the latter of which he had been forced to use his sword, *The King Maker*, to finish off.

He desired to clean both himself and his trusted weapon much more than he desired to ruminate on his aunt's concerns about his lack of mate. And he could see Wolf Lake, which bordered his village, glittering in the distance.

"It seems we have caught the King of Wolves unawares," a voice said from behind him.

Fenris stopped short, his grip tightening around the hilt of his sword, before he turned to face his cousin, Vidar, a wolf almost as tall and broad as he. Fenris had banished Vidar from their village two moons ago, after the younger wolf had beaten and attempted to couple with a household servant girl who did not wish his advances.

Vidar had thought his position as cousin to the king would keep him protected, despite the strict laws against coupling with a she-wolf without her father's consent. And indeed, it had pained Fenris greatly to banish a family member who shared his own longhouse. But in the end, even Fenris could not hold himself above wolf law, especially the ones he had set down himself during the bloody years he had spent reaffirming his position as the king of the North wolves.

But like a recurring dream, Vidar now once again stood before him. However, this time, his battle axe, which Fenris had allowed him to keep, was raised and his eyes were shining with hatred and malice. Also, this time he did not stand in front of Fenris alone. At various points behind him stood four other men with swords, three of which Fenris recognized as wolves he had banished from their village for crimes ranging from theft to the murder of humans, which were also strictly forbidden under both his laws.

Fenris raised his own sword. "You should not be so close to my village, Cousin. Your mother might see you and you have already well disappointed her."

"I beheld you talking to the wicked sorceress." He bared his sharp lupine teeth. "The one who did put that harlot servant to her false accusation."

Though his aunt had been the one to bring the servant girl to Fenris, it had taken but one look at the badly beaten girl to assess what had happened. He knew her attacker to be Vidar, who he had spied watching the yellow-haired girl with hard *losti*—lust— in his eyes on several occasions. The extent of his crime against a girl who many in his household considered like a family member had been enough to sicken even his mother's sister, Esja, Vidar's own mother. She had yet to ask her nephew to reverse his decision, even though it was known by all that Vidar had only gone as far as the mountains on the northern side of the lake to live.

"What matter of business is this, Vidar?" he asked.

"I wish to once again take my place in our village and there is but one way to do that." Vidar stopped smiling now. "Become the new alpha king."

Fenris shook his head. "You cannot hope to best me on your own."

There was a reason the Alpha King title had stayed in his line for five generations. The sons of Fenris were known throughout the Northern lands as fierce warriors, and he himself had been trained from childhood to defend his inherited crown.

Vidar grinned. "Not on my own, no. But my friends have avowed to herald it that way when we return to the village with your severed head in my hand."

"No one will believe your tale."

"It does not matter that they believe, only that they submit to their new king."

Fenris spat. Vidar had been a pig's penis since childhood, prone to tantrums and high-handed with his mother and two sisters. And now it was plain to see he had gone mad with desire for power and revenge.

Fenris considered himself a warrior of great skill, but even he could not best five wolves, especially having just come off the late winter hunt. He cursed himself for letting his mind become so distracted by the conversation with his aunt that he had momentarily relaxed his guard, giving his cousin the perfect opening for this underhanded attack.

The conversation with his aunt.

Fenris lowered the hand that held his sword and raised the one that held the rag with the spell written upon it.

Mistaking the lowering of his sword as an admittance of defeat, Vidar came charging toward him with his battle axe raised high.

Fenris barely had enough time to utter the words that would send him hurtling through a gate to the gods-only-knew—but at that moment, any land was better than this plain, surrounded by power-mad Vidar and his outlaw followers.

He did not hear the gate open behind him, but knew it must

have, because Vidar came to a fumbling stop, his eyes widening and his mouth falling open.

In the next moment, Fenris was sucked backward into a pitch-black tunnel of wind, which sent his body hurtling through space and time at such a speed, he barely managed to hold on to his sword.

Eventually he was deposited on a snowy plateau, his head slamming against a large rock just as he hit the ground with a bone-crunching thud. His head spun, and he groaned in a bid to stay conscious, but it was a bid not won. And he was surround by blackness again.

The sound of two voices speaking a strange language above him eventually came filtering in through the new blackness. And when he opened his eyes he found what looked like a Moor standing above him with his booted foot on his chest.

Fenris moved quickly. Even though the man was dressed in a strange costume—some manner of faded blue trousers and a thin coat made of a shiny and slick material Fenris had never seen before—he could smell that the man was a fellow wolf. Consequently, he didn't waste time trying to deduce who this wolf was or why he had his boot planted on his chest. His way had always been to kill quickly, and his own life had been spared many times over because he did so. In a few moves, he reversed their positions and had raised his sword for the killing blow—

"No!!!!"

What sounded like a female's voice rang out beside him. And he would have ignored it, except...his nostrils flared...he could not.

As if compelled by an invisible puppet master, he turned toward the voice, and found a trembling she-wolf with bushy hair and what looked like some manner of weapon pointed at him. Perhaps the spell had transported him to Iberia or what he'd heard referred to as *Blaland*, a hot and dry land to the far south where *blamenn*, black people with very dark skin, lived.

It was she.

Whoever she was, wherever she hailed from, he recognized her for who she was the instant his eyes met hers. Not only from her intoxicating scent, but also from his body's reaction to her. A powerful wave of desire overtook Fenris, causing him to sway, even though he was in a firm killing stance. His cock swelled inside his hunting trousers, hard and surprisingly insistent, as if he were a pup in his first stages of coming manhood.

For a moment, he stood there frozen, unable to move, he was so enthralled by her. But finally he remembered himself enough to say, "I am here for you." He held up the rag with the spell upon it. "And now we must speak these words as one, so I might go back to my lands and vanquish my enemy."

She looked from side to side, before spewing forth words that sounded to him vaguely like some form of Germanic, but not a dialect he recognized. Why would this dark woman be speaking to him in Germanic?

He started toward her, which seemed to alarm her. She made a high-pitched noise, like a mouse, before squeezing her eyes closed. A whistling sound then emitted from her strange weapon right before something struck him with the sting of a fierce insect bite.

He looked down to see some manner of dart sticking from his shoulder. And just as he moved to pull it out, a powerful sleep overtook him, one he could not resist, even though he strove hard to fight the enveloping blackness.

CHAPTER THREE

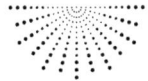

"YOU know, if we were mated that wouldn't have gone so bad," Rafe said, a couple of hours after the confrontation at the portal.

It had been an awkward and unwieldy business getting the large maybe-Viking down the mountain to the town's two-room clinic. But he now lie sleeping upright in a hospital bed, to which he'd been handcuffed, looking much more peaceful than the two people in the room's side-by-side visitor chairs.

Chloe adjusted her position to look at Rafe with an incredulous blink. "Seriously? We are in the clinic with a *possibly crazed Viking* sleeping off a tranq, and this is what you want to talk about?"

Rafe shrugged as if time-traveling Viking werewolves happened every day. "Once we're mated, we'll be telepathically connected, too, which means we'll be able to say things like, 'Hey, Chloe, don't talk to him in German, just shoot him already.'"

"Or things like, 'Hey, Rafe, you can thank me for saving your life any day now.'"

Rafe clenched his jaw and looked away. "The truth is, I'm more pissed at myself for letting him get the upper hand. I shouldn't have let my guard down. What if he had hurt you, or worse? I wouldn't have been able to live with myself."

He sounded so guilty that Chloe's irritation was instantly replaced with the need to comfort him. She placed a hand on his arm. "But he didn't hurt me or you. That's all that matters."

Rafe shook his head. "I've never seen a guy that big move so fast. I wonder what he did to get cast out of wherever he came from."

So did Chloe.

Doc Fischer, their shifter town's middle-aged and perennially cranky doctor, entered the room at that moment. "Has he tried to tell you why he got sent back yet?"

"No, he's still not awake," Chloe said.

The doctor screwed his up his craggy face. "What do you mean? He's wide awake."

They whipped their heads around to see the maybe-Viking lying there with his eyes wide open and staring at them. Hard.

Doc Fischer went to his bed-side and Rafe joined him. However, Chloe chose that moment to get out of the doctor's way, repositioning herself on the opposite side of the room from the reluctant patient. As much as she had enjoyed meeting the werewolves who came through the gate in the past, she figured it was largely because they were *she-wolves* from different cultures or points in history—but blood-thirsty werewolves with swords? Nah, she wasn't so into that.

This guy had come very close to killing her best friend. And somehow his prone position and the fact that he was handcuffed to the bed by both hands didn't make him seem any less deadly. For whatever reason, Chloe was having trouble staying calm now that he was awake. Something about him caused her insides to go all skittery. It was similar to how she felt when Rafe tried to talk to her about their heat night, but with a side dish of electric fear that made her nerves tingle.

And she only became more unsettled when his intense gaze followed her in her attempt to put space between them.

"We figure he's a criminal and got cast out of his pack. Maybe he challenged the alpha and this was his punishment," Rafe told Doc Fisher, after the old man finished examining the maybe-Viking's eyes with a pen-light.

The doctor frowned. "Hmm, you say he came through the gate un-shifted? Usually a gate banishment is done on a diseased wolf or in desperation and toward the apex of a fight. He doesn't have any wounds, except some bruising where his head hit that rock."

Rafe shrugged. "Maybe he had a trial and was found guilty. There were a few packs that used the trial system, right?"

"Actually, I just consulted on this case with a friend of mine at UC Denver who specializes in history and literature from the Viking period. He said Norway and Iceland were known for their strict legal system during the Viking Age, which is why he doesn't think this is a gate banishment. According to him, they had a fairly thorough punishment system in place, no need to go wild with the gates."

"Then maybe he's not a Viking. He could be from some other place and time and we just didn't recognize whatever language he's speaking."

The doctor shook his head. "I don't think so. I sent a picture of that sword of his to my professor friend and he recognized it, because of the wolf on the hilt. He even sent me a picture. It's on display at the Museum of Cultural History in Oslo. They don't have a firm history on it. But it definitely dates back to the Viking Age."

Doc Fischer re-pocketed his pen-light. "I think we might need to apply Occam's razor here."

A bad feeling began to brew in Chloe's stomach.

"What do you mean?" Rafe asked.

"You know, 'the simplest explanation is probably the most

likely one?'" The doctor clasped his hands in front of him like a lawyer about to put forth his case. "He came through the gate unshifted with no visible wounds. You said he tried to kill you but stopped because Chloe told him not to."

"Not because I told him not to," Chloe said. "It was more like I took him by surprise."

Doc Fischer gave her skeptical look. "Plus, he hasn't taken his eyes off of you, despite the fact that he's handcuffed down to a bed in a time period clearly not his own. I'm thinking the logical conclusion here is this Viking has come forward in time for his fated mate."

Both Chloe and Rafe gaped at him.

"And it's Chloe," the doctor added, just in case they weren't getting his original meaning.

"No," Chloe and Rafe said at the same time.

Doc Fischer turned his no-nonsense gaze on Chloe. "Chloe is there something you want to tell us?"

"No," answered Chloe, her eyes going wide with indignation.

The doctor picked up the maybe-Viking's chart and started making notes. "So you don't feel anything at all right now for this wolf? No increased heart rate, heightened arousal, anything like that?"

"No! I don't feel anything for him." Chloe looked to the red-haired man who was still quite openly staring at her but then she quickly had to cut her eyes away, because she wasn't lying, but she wasn't exactly telling the truth either. While she was definitely not aroused when she looked at him, the weird skittery feeling did get worse.

"Look, we're all thinking he's probably a Viking, right?" she said. "The last time I checked, there weren't a ton of black people in Norway back then. For all we know, this guy has never seen a black girl, and that's why he's staring at me."

She turned to Rafe, hoping he'd back her up as he did in most things.

But Rafe didn't agree. In fact his eyes burned with suspicion as he came to stand in front of her. He slowly and deliberately sniffed the air around her, and only then did he visibly calm down. "I don't smell any arousal on her," he said, his voice angry with the declaration. He swung his gaze back to the doctor. "I don't like what you're insinuating, Doc."

The doctor held his hands up. "Don't kill the messenger. I'm only checking off all the possibilities."

Rafe glared at him. "I won't let you insult her like that. She's my mate."

"Not yet, she isn't. Not officially." The doctor shook his head. "And it's not an insult. I'm older than both of you, and I know you two love each other, but . . ." He paused, seeming to search for the right words. "These things happen. More often then you think. Especially among wolves. There's a reason all of our legends involve either great alpha fights or tragic love stories. North American wolves have only strayed away from the tradition of fated mates spells in the last two hundred years, which is relatively recent if you think about it in terms of world history. You need to realize it can still be quite powerful when one is cast."

"Well, that's not what's happening here," Rafe informed him. "He's a criminal, and even if he's not shifted, that doesn't mean he wasn't banished for something."

Chloe was having a hard time figuring out how she should be reacting to this conversation. Though she was happy Rafe decided to come to her defense—eventually—the longer he discussed this topic with Doc Fischer, the more nervous and on edge she felt. Plus, she could still feel the maybe-Viking's eyes burning hot on her, which made her feel even more awkward.

"All right, if you say so. I mean, you're the alpha prince," Doc Fischer answered. It was impossible not to hear the insincerity in his words. He might as well have said, "You're being unreasonable, but I'll just go ahead and agree with you because you're the entitled alpha prince."

And apparently Rafe sensed his real meaning, too, because he said, "I'll prove it. If he came back here for Chloe, then he'd go ape if I kissed her in front of him, right?"

The doctor nodded. "Yes, he's her fated mate, he'd definitely 'go ape' as you call it."

Rafe turned to her and cupped her shoulders. Chloe immediately felt her body tense.

"It's okay," Rafe said. "I know you don't like public displays of affection, but this is for a good cause."

This didn't soothe Chloe any. The truth was, she had told Rafe early in their engagement she didn't like kissing in front of other people, but that had been an excuse to keep their make-out sessions contained. Rafe was outrageously handsome, and she loved talking with him and laughing with him and hugging him and even cuddling with him. However, kissing him gave her a slight case of the heebie-jeebies, and she had to not only brace herself for his kisses, but also concentrate on something else altogether in order to keep it from showing. More than one *Black Mountain Woman* blog post had been completely composed in her head, while she forced herself to make out with Rafe.

But in this case, she didn't really have time to fully brace herself before his lips fell on hers. And she immediately set all her attention to fighting the weird urge to rip her lips away from his that always overtook her when they were intimate. However, less than a few seconds into the wildly uncomfortable kiss, they were interrupted by a loud clanging sound.

Rafe pulled away from the kiss, which allowed her to see the source of the sound. It was the maybe-Viking. He was thrashing in the bed, and the handcuffs clanged against the bed's metal railing, he was straining so hard to break free. His face had turned red with anger, and she could actually see the veins in his neck. And that was before he started spewing his strange language, directing several words toward Rafe that Chloe was fairly sure involved some really harsh threats and expletives.

Seeing this display of temper paralyzed Chloe, rooting her in place. But Doc Fischer, who held degrees in both medical and veterinary science and had apparently seen it all, lazily prepared a syringe before stepping forward and plunging it into the maybe Viking's arm without a word.

The sedative only took a few moments to take hold, but the maybe Viking fought his restraints the entire time, his eyes bulging and locked on Rafe as he cursed in his foreign language, his face screwed up with rage, until eventually his words began to slur and he fell back against the bed in another heavy sleep.

After he passed out, Doc Fischer regarded them both with the cynical aplomb. "Well, I think that answers our question."

CHAPTER FOUR

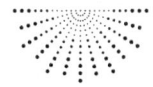

FOR as long as Chloe could remember, she had wanted to be part of the Nightwolf family. She could still remember the three weeks she'd spent in their family's mansion after being found by the side of the road, shivering and alone. The wolf law of every state was that the king had to take in any abandoned children left in his province, which she later figured out was why her parents had chosen to abandon her in this particular place.

Back then, the clan only placed wolves with families of the same race. So though most abandoned children her age were placed in three days or less, it took three whole weeks to find her a home. And they were three of the best weeks of her entire life. Even at the age of four, Rafe had been charming and awesome. Two seconds after she stepped through the door, he had immediately asked her to come up and play in his toy room, which was just what it sounded like, a room larger than the entire one-bedroom apartment she had shared with her parents. It was designated for all of Rafe's toys, and he'd been more than happy to share with her.

She also instantly loved Rafe's parents. His father had a booming laugh and considered himself a friend to all—as long as they were Broncos fans. Luckily she had answered with a tentative, "Yes?" when he'd asked her at their first meeting, "You cheer for the Broncos, little girl?" And Rafe's mother was warm and nurturing in a way her own had never been, hugging her often and assuring her everything would be all right.

When three weeks passed and they had only been able to find Myrna Adams, a local black spinster, to take her in, Chloe had actually been grateful. She wouldn't be with a family of her own, but at least she'd stay close to the family she now loved the most.

And a year later when she and Rafe entered kindergarten at Wolf Springs Elementary, the only all-wolf public school in Colorado, they'd picked up right back where they started, playing together every day, and soon she and Myrna became regulars at their Sunday dinners. She had grown up with Rafe, and when he proposed to her, it felt like he was not only asking her to be his mate, but also inviting her into his loving, close-knit family, which she wanted more than anything.

Over the pass few years, she had prayed and prayed for her heat night to come, not just so she'd feel more comfortable kissing Rafe, but also so she could take her official place as part of his family and even start one of her own with him. There was nothing in this world she wanted more.

So when some random time-travelling, maybe-Viking werewolf showed up out of the blue all but saying out loud that she was his fated mate, it felt like nothing short of getting stabbed.

"No," she said, finally meeting his eyes. "We are not... we are *not* fated mates."

The maybe Viking stilled in his thrashing and stared back at her, his own eyes softening as if the sound of her voice alone was enough to calm him down.

"Did you lie to me?" Rafe asked, dropping his hands from her arms.

"No!" she said again, turning back to him. "I would never do that."

The Rafe she knew, the laid back and reasonable one with a great sense of humor, was gone now and in his place was a stranger, with a voice so distinctly hard, it felt like the only thing in the room. "Did you know who he was from the beginning?"

She reached for him, catching his rigid arms beneath her trembling hands, "No, Rafe, I had no idea he thought he was here for me."

He glared at her. "Do you want to mate with him? Do you want to start kissing him in public?"

"No, no, no!" She shook her head with frantic denial. "I swear I don't. I swear I had no idea. I would never lie to you. You're my best friend, and I love you more than anyone else in this world. Please believe me. I feel nothing for him. Nothing."

Rafe's face remained impassive as he sniffed the air around her, his nostrils flaring wide.

"She's not aroused," he said to Doc Fischer. "Wouldn't she be aroused if he were her fated mate?"

Relief coursed through Chloe like a river through the desert. The cold stranger had gone and her Rafe was back, once again defending her, just as he had when they were kids and the wolves in their class made fun of her for being a foster pup.

Doc Fischer gave them a long, considering look before saying, "In rare cases, a fated mate can catch the scent of someone who doesn't return his feelings. Those situations usually get messy and end up with the two males fighting for dominance."

Rafe set his jaw. "I will be more than happy to put his ass down if that's what it comes to."

"Now, now, calm down, young wolf," the doctor said. He pulled out his smart phone. "I'm going to call back my friend at UC Denver. Maybe if I get him up here, he can help us out with this language barrier and we can figure this out without any wolves having to lose their lives."

"Call your friend," Rafe said, alpha prince to his very core.

"But I'm letting you know right now, if he tries to lay one hand on Chloe, it's not going to end peacefully."

The doctor gave Chloe a sullen look, as if this entire situation were all her fault as opposed to some unfair trick of fate. But he eventually answered Rafe. "Noted. Now get out of here, I've got some calls to make if we want to get this situation resolved before tomorrow's full moon."

※

She wasn't aroused by the Viking, and she hadn't lied to Rafe about not feeling anything sexual whatsoever for the strange visitor. If anything, the whole situation had turned her nether regions even more numb. Before, there had been the loud absence of any kind of sexual feeling on her part. But now she was feeling the opposite of aroused, like she'd rather hike up a thousand King's Trails than have sex with anyone, ever. That's how horrible the scene back in the clinic had been.

But still, guilt clawed at her insides as Rafe walked her home from the clinic. People kept stopping him to ask who had come through the portal this time.

"Is it true it was a man?" their high school Social Studies teacher asked. "Mercedes Griswold said she saw you two carrying a man's body into the clinic. Is he dead? Did you have to kill him like your dad had to kill that rabid wolf back in the day?"

Rafe handled all the questions diplomatically, with various versions of, "We're not allowed to talk about it just yet, but we'll be making an announcement soon." The answer sounded neutral enough, but Chloe knew him too well not to recognize the edge in his voice as he answered question after question about their mysterious visitor.

"You don't have to walk me home," she told him. "It's been a long day and I know you probably want to catch up at your office."

Along with his duties as the alpha prince of Colorado, Rafe was also the vice president of Wolf Springs Timber, one of the largest privately owned logging companies in the world. It was rare for him to take lunch, much less a whole half-day off work.

"You said you were going to do a chicken recipe for your next show. Doesn't that mean you need me to kill the chicken?" he asked.

She wrung her hands together. "You know what, I'm going to try to kill the chicken myself this time. It's so ridiculous that I always have to call you to do it for me."

"That's what mates are for," Rafe said, his voice flat. "We help each other out when we need it."

"Sure, sure," Chloe answered. "But what kind of werewolf can't bear to kill a chicken? It's so embarrassing."

"Not as embarrassing as what just happened in the clinic," he answered.

And there it was. Rafe never had been the sort to dance around the elephant in the room.

"I'm sorry that happened," she said. "I have no idea why the fated mates spell would send that guy forward in time for me, especially since I feel no connection to him whatsoever. You believe me, right?"

He stopped and studied her face for a few moments before deciding out loud, "I do."

"And if it comes down to a choice between you and him, I pick you, Rafe."

"I know."

"You're my best friend."

Now something unreadable passed over his face. "You keep on saying that."

"What?"

"That I'm your best friend. You've said it like five times today. But you know what I call you when I talk about you? My mate."

And just when she thought things couldn't get any more

awkward. "I call you that, too," she insisted. "And what does it matter what I call you anyway? The most important thing is I love you. I love you so much, more than anybody else in this entire world."

"I believe you. But this Viking thing..."

She grabbed his hand. "Look, Rafe, if you want to have sex before I go into heat, that's fine with me. I don't care what Council law says. I'm twenty-five, old enough to make my own decisions." Including the decision to ignore the wrenching of her own stomach as she made this offer.

Rafe rubbed the side of his face with his knuckles, considering. But then he said, "No, I'm an alpha prince. I can't ignore the law."

A wave of relief swept over her. She could have forced herself to hold still for sex with Rafe, just like she forced herself to accept his kisses, but it wouldn't have been pleasant at all. For what felt like the millionth time, she sent up a tiny prayer that going into heat would solve everything between them and finally help her body catch up with her heart. She-wolves were actually known for their lusty nature, and she'd seen nerdy and mousy girls from her high school honors classes transform into black leather-wearing, unapologetic sexpots with just one moon cycle and mating. She hoped to God it would be the same for her.

But out loud to Rafe, she said, "Okay, if that's the way you feel, we won't break Council law. I just want you to know how committed I am to you, to us, to our being together and starting a family."

"I know you are." Rafe took her hand in his and began walking again. "But you know how the wolves gossip. We're not going to be able to keep this a secret for long."

She shook her head. "There's nothing to hide. He thinks I'm his fated mate, but I'm with you. Tomorrow, we'll have Doc Fischer's professor friend explain that to him, and he'll go back to whatever time period he came from. The end."

"How about if he challenges me?" Rafe asks.

"There's nothing to challenge if I say no-go. This isn't the dark ages when she-wolves didn't have any say over who claimed them."

"We could move in together."

This time she was the one who stopped walking. "Wait, what?"

Rafe ran a hand through his dark locks. "Listen, I didn't tell you this…because it's bullshit. You know how much my dad likes you, but he kind of thinks you haven't gone into heat because you're not really in love with me."

Her eyes narrowed. "What? That's not even how it works. It's purely physiological. Like getting your period. It happens when it happens. Doc Fischer says she-wolves can go into heat as late as their thirties."

"I know what Doc Fischer says," Rafe said. "But Dad's old-school. He's not buying it. And he's the Colorado alpha. So if this guy steps up, claiming you as his fated mate, and you're not even physically living with me, he might pull the king card and say we can't get married."

Chloe studied his face and knew this wasn't really a hypothetical they were discussing. Rafe was telling her the king was so upset about how long they'd been engaged, he would pull rank in order to end it if he had the right opportunity.

"I wouldn't let him get away with it," Rafe assured her, reading her mind as best friends did. "If he tries to pull that shit, I'll run away with you before I let him tear us apart. But I don't want it to come to that."

She clamped her lips together. "I don't want it to come to that either. And you know, even if your dad said we couldn't get married, that doesn't mean I'm going to marry some weird, blood-thirsty Viking who came through the portal. It's either you or nobody for me."

"Look at you, getting all angry and defending our love." Rafe smiled down at her. "I like this side of you. There might be a little wolf in you yet."

He pulled her into his arms and Chloe nuzzled her face into his chest, her she-wolf loving the way it felt to be packed in close to another body.

It was a very sweet moment until Rafe said, "But think about moving in with me, okay? I mean, we're going to do it after your heat night anyway, so why wait?"

Her face fell. "Actually, I was hoping you'd move in with me."

"My place is bigger, " he pointed out. "Four bedrooms. You've only got two. Plus, I didn't buy the house for you to stay there. The plan was to move you out and move somebody else in, so we can start receiving rent on it."

"Yeah, but…" She tried to figure out a nice way to tell him she'd rather live in the small, cozy cabin which was set up just the way she liked it for her Black Mountain Woman videos, than his man cave of a house with flat screens in every room, including the bathroom and kitchen.

But she already knew what he'd say. This was Rafe. He'd offer to remodel the kitchen and get rid of its small flat screen if it really bothered her that much. But he'd resent her for it. He'd never understood why she preferred to live like a homesteader as opposed to a modern woman in the modern ages, and it was hard to explain the draw of the lifestyle to someone who liked his electronic toys as much as Rafe did.

But ever since Myrna had first taught her to sew on her ancient Singer, she had felt drawn to the idea of doing everything herself. Making her own clothes, her own food, her own just-about-everything and never having to depend on others to provide for her again. Still as passionate as she was about how she chose to live, she didn't like the idea of getting into a lifestyle battle with Rafe any sooner than she had to.

"Can I think about it?" she asked, when what she really meant was. "Can you give me some time to figure out how to save our engagement, keep you from falling out with your father, and get rid of the Viking who thinks I'm his fated mate without having to move in with you before my heat night?"

"Sure," he said. An apologetic smile settled on his face. "Listen, I'm sorry we're having to deal with this bullshit. I wish we hadn't been the ones to go up there. Sometimes, I wish I weren't the alpha prince of Colorado. It would be nice to be a normal wolf with normal problems that my dad would judge on a fair basis, not because I'm his son. If this were happening to any other couple, it wouldn't even be a question of who he'd side with."

When they reached his house they parted with another hug. As she watched Rafe walk away, she remembered his proposal in the high school gymnasium, just two weeks after Myrna died as if he couldn't bear the thought of her being alone in this world again like she was when they first met. He really was her best friend, and she couldn't lose him, which meant she had to get rid of the maybe-Viking, whatever it took. The consequences of not doing so were just too scary to even think about. She didn't know if she could mentally survive being a lone wolf again.

CHAPTER FIVE

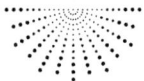

"YOU'VE got to be kidding me," Chloe all but yelled into her cell phone the next day.

"Listen, kid, my nurse is off on full moon days and the guy smells like animal blood. He's stinking up the entire clinic, and he needs a sponge bath."

"Then why can't you do it?" Chloe asked.

"Because I'm on the road to Denver to pick up my professor friend, who doesn't drive. And also, because he's *your* fated mate."

Chloe gritted her teeth. "He's not my anything. I am one hundred percent with Rafe."

"Okay, well then because he's the werewolf who came over one thousand years into the future just to find you. Is that any better?"

"No," she grumbled.

"Well, here's the deal, kid. You and Rafe asked me to keep this situation under wraps, so unless you want me to ask your fiancé to do it, I suggest you get down here and clean this guy up. And get him some new clothes while you're at it."

And that was how Chloe ended up abandoning her preparations for her chicken and fennel episode of *Black Mountain*

Woman, and running to the local general store to pick up a pair of extra-large basketball shorts, men's underwear, and a Wolf Springs T-shirt for the man who had turned her life upside down in less than twelve hours.

Doc Fischer was right about being able to smell him as soon as you walked in the door, but it was Chloe's opinion he had exaggerated how bad it was. He did smell of some animal whose scent she didn't recognize off the top of her head, but it didn't overwhelm his real smell, which she actually found quite pleasant. It was a mixture of smoke, evergreens, ocean, wind, and mountain that made her think of outdoor barbecues and ski vacations.

In any case, she was happy he was still out cold when she arrived in his room with the clothes and a basin, which she filled with warm water. She washed his face first, running the warm cloth over it and wondering what he looked like under his thick beard. She already knew his eyes were light gray and she could see his nose was long and straight, but the red beard and his tangled lion's mane of a hair-do pretty much hid every other feature.

Next she added soap to the water in the basin, before dipping the towel in again and running it over his chest, doing her best not to admire the hard muscles she felt underneath her cloth. Whatever this guy did for a living wherever he was from, it had gifted him with a beautiful body. She had to put some effort into lifting his arms, which were so thick with muscle that getting underneath them in order to wash his arm pits was a bit of a challenge.

Somewhat out of breath, she emptied out the water and refilled it with a fresh batch of warm, soapy water. Now she had to do his bottom half.

Once again she had to put a lot of effort into getting him clean. First she had to tug off his pants, which didn't have any fasteners on them, so she had to roll them down his hips—

quickly averting her eyes when she saw he wasn't wearing any underwear underneath. She kept her eyes averted, washing around his groin area as best she could without actually looking at it. Still that didn't keep her heart from just about jumping out of her chest when something long and thick thumped against her arm, like a baton of flesh-covered steel.

Her eyes flew to the maybe-Viking to see if he was awake, but he slept on, apparently unaware of what the lower half of his body was up to.

Chloe finished up with that particular area as quickly as she could, her head turned away, then tugged the underwear and basketball shorts on him—no small feat but worth it if it meant covering up his sleeping erection. She wished she also cover up his chest, but he was chained to the bed, which meant she wouldn't be able to get his arms through it. So she just put that item on the bedside table, and replaced the now cold water in the bowl.

A few minutes later, she silently cheered when she reached his long and wide feet, giving each a few quick swipes with her towel. All done, and now she could just tip-toe on out of the room, without the maybe-Viking never even knowing she was there.

But then, suddenly, that same skittery feeling from the day before overtook her and her stomach sank. Sure enough, when she looked up, she found the Viking wide-awake and staring at her with enough heat in his eyes to melt all the snow on the nearby mountain.

❋

*F*enris came awake slowly blinking against the bright light. His body was still heavy with whatever potion he had been given, but for some reason, his manhood was now swollen and constricted in some manner of binding he did not know. Despite this, soft waves of languid pleasure were coursing through his body, starting at his legs.

He turned his eyes in the direction of the pleasurable sensation and found his fated mate, the dark beauty from the day before, giving him, of all things, a bath.

She was once again dressed in a strange costume, some manner of wool tunic top, dyed a pale blue that covered her neck and arms but squeezed her chest in such a way that left little doubt a heavy bosom rested beneath it's confines. In his land, it was forbidden for both she-wolves and human woman to wear the clothing of men. But her legs were encased in tight black men's trousers that framed her shapely hips and made him want to rut her where she stood, even if he could smell that she hadn't yet had her first heat. A strange notion within itself, since she had quite obviously come into her womanhood.

On this day, she wore her bushy hair tied to the side in a long braid that fell all the way to her bounteous breasts. He reached out to touch it, so different from his own, but then he remembered anew that he had been tied to the railing of a strange, mechanical bed with some manner of metal, which somehow held him fast despite it's light and thin nature.

He once again rattled the bed in a bid to free himself.

But the dark beauty shook her head, frantically speaking to him in her strange dialect, before coming around the bed and laying her hands on his chest.

Her touch immediately calmed him, and soon he found himself falling back against the bed's soft pillows, his desire to be free of his bonds replaced with the desire to gaze upon her great beauty.

She tried to pull away from him then, but he covered her hands with his own, keeping her there.

"Nay, stay here, maiden," he said, even though he had gleaned by now that she could not understand his tongue any better than he understood hers.

"Stay here," he repeated in a whisper, gazing into her wary brown eyes, as he allowed himself to absorb the warmth of her hands on his naked chest, and enjoy the sight of her own chest heaving up and down with quickened breaths.

Then he leaned forward and took the kiss he had been wanting from her since first their eyes met.

For a moment she acquiesced to his kiss, but then she suddenly pulled away, her face aghast as she said something else in her tongue and tried to reclaim her hands from his.

He did not let go at first, and perhaps would have kept her there for a few more sweet kisses, except he suddenly smelled another presence in the room. His smile faded when he looked up and found the wolf from yesterday standing in the doorway. The same wolf who had dared touch what was his.

❋

For what had to be at least the tenth time that day, Chloe cursed the fates that had brought her to this situation. When the maybe-Viking had started rattling the bed again in his attempt to get out of the handcuffs, she had placed her hands on his chest more out of instinct than plan.

"Stop. You've got to calm down," she'd said. To her surprise he'd obeyed her command, instantly calming down, the expression on his face replaced by a look so soft, it sent an unbidden jolt of electricity through her stomach. One she didn't like at all.

She tried to pull her hands away, but he kept her there, speaking softly in his strange language with a smile that crinkled his eyes and made him look way more handsome than she'd thought he was while she was bathing him.

And then the next thing she knew, he was kissing her. She'd been so surprised by the feel of his lips moving over hers and by the complete lack of heebie-jeebies on her part, that she just froze, all of her senses momentarily overwhelmed.

But then she remembered herself and pulled away from him. "Let go," she said.

He didn't, only gripped her hands tighter. But then his eyes hardened as he gazed at something beyond her shoulder. Even if her sense of smell hadn't chosen that moment to come back online, she would have known just from the look on his face it was Rafe standing in the doorway.

This time she yanked on her hands so hard, they slipped out of the maybe-Viking's grip, and even then she only just managed to get in front of Rafe before he leaped toward the hospital bed, looking like he was set to tear its occupant apart with his bare hands.

"Rafe, no," she said, pushing him backwards before he could.

"You were kissing him," Rafe said, the words thick and feral in his throat.

"No, he kissed me, and it took me by surprise. I didn't kiss him back."

"All the more reason for me to kill him," Rafe said.

"Rafe, please. It was nothing. You have to calm down." He was pushing so hard to get past her, Chloe was half afraid he'd take her out just to get at the other wolf. And if that wasn't enough, she could hear the bed rattling behind them, which meant the maybe-Viking was once again trying to free himself to get to Rafe.

Luckily, just when her arms were about to give, Doc Fischer and a stringy man in a tweed blazer walked in. They quickly assessed the situation and took over restraining Rafe, each grabbing him by one of his long arms.

"Now calm down, son," Doc Fischer said, his voice quiet but firm. "If you're going to try to take him out every time my back is turned, then I'm going to have to make you wait outside."

The maybe-Viking chose that moment to start spitting words of challenge and insult at Rafe, which needed no translation. And

Rafe jerked forward, all but frothing at the mouth in his effort to get to him.

In the end, Doc Fischer and the professor had to drag Rafe out and lock the clinic door so he couldn't get back in.

It was all Chloe could do to hold back tears of frustration as she watched them toss Rafe out like some derelict. And even after they locked the door, she could hear her fiancé, who normally tried so hard to hold himself in a manner befitting an alpha prince, yelling like a mad man outside the building.

"Well, so much for keeping this situation a secret," Doc Fischer said. "As loud as that got, the whole town probably knows what's going on now."

"I should go to him," Chloe said, heading toward the door.

But Doc Fischer stopped her with a shake of his head. "No, young lady, you should sit down. Whatever your fated mate has to say, you should hear it, too."

"Rafe is my mate," she said, "You admitted it yourself. I'm not aroused, so the attraction must be one-sided."

"No, I said in *rare* cases, a fated mate catches the scent of someone who doesn't return his feelings. I didn't talk about what happens when she-wolves mate with other wolves only to have a fated mate come along and try to claim her. But I'm telling you now, it rarely ends well. Half the time the she-wolf runs away with her fated mate, sometimes even leaving her pups behind. The other half of the time her current mate has to kill the fated one in order to make him leave her alone. For your sake, I also didn't mention in front of your fiancé that I suspect the only reason you're able to resist this wolf is because you haven't gone into heat yet, and who knows how much longer that will last?"

"I would never—"

Doc Fischer interrupted her with a snort and a roll of his eyes. "I hate when young wolves try to tell me what they'd 'never' do. The truth is you have no idea what you'd do until you actually go into heat like a regular she-wolf would have years ago. And God help you if your fated mate is here when you finally do." He pointed at the guest chair. "Now if you're serious about telling this guy you don't want him and sending him back through the portal, sit down so we can get this over with."

She crossed her arms over her chest and sat. She didn't like Doc Fischer insinuating she would leave the man she loved the most in this world for some stranger she'd only met the day before, but he was right about one thing. It was better to just get this over with. The sooner they did, the sooner she could go to Rafe. He'd quieted down, but she could still sense his presence outside the clinic, furious, hurt, and brooding.

The professor tentatively stepped into the angry silence of her acquiescence. He looked to be around the same age as Doc Fischer, but had the nebbish quality male wolves who never claimed mates tended to get. He was tall and skinny, and though he didn't wear glasses, since all werewolves had better than twenty/twenty vision, it looked like he ought to be.

"Hi, I'm Professor Henley," he said with a small wave. "I teach Viking Studies at the university. Normally I wouldn't risk travel on a full moon night, but I couldn't pass up this opportunity."

He turned to the Viking, who had calmed after they ejected Rafe and now sat watching all of them, his eyes glittering with what looked like a combination of anger, frustration, and curiosity.

"The sword I saw out in the lobby and the fact that he was yelling at your... ah, friend in Old Norse tells me he's a Viking," the professor said, running his eyes over the large man as if he were a majestic sight indeed. "Also, his hair is red. It's rumored the Norwegian Viking wolves all had 'hair like fire.' And quite a few of my fellow werewolf history professors believe Erik the Red to have been a werewolf.'" He reached out, as if to touch the Viking's hair, but pulled back at the last moment, probably sensing correctly that this wasn't the type of man who would appreciate being petted.

"Thanks for the history lesson," Doc Fischer said. "Can you talk to him or what?"

The professor held up an Old Norse-English dictionary. "Well, I've only used Old Norse in the context of translating or reciting poems and certain texts from that age, but I'll do my best."

The professor cleared his throat before hawking up a few words of Old Norse.

The Viking's eyes widened in surprise, and he answered with a few words of his own, which caused the professor's own eyes to widen.

He turned back to her and Doc Fischer. "He says he's called Fenris. Do you know what that means?"

They both shook their heads. "Fenris is the Norse wolf god, the one all Norwegian werewolves believed themselves to be descended from. Only wolves in the alpha line are given this name."

"Wait, wait, wait," Chloe said, holding up her hands. "Are you're trying to tell me this guy is also an alpha prince like Rafe?"

The professor asked the Viking another question in the harsh language.

And this time the Viking looked at her when he answered.

The professor gave a nervous laugh, before translating. "No, he's not an alpha prince. He just commanded me to tell you he is king of the North wolves. He say he's come to this strange place to fetch you and he's ready to take you home with him."

The Viking continued to stare at her as he spoke one more word, which the professor immediately translated. "Now."

CHAPTER SIX

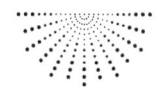

IT took Chloe quite a few shocked moments before she was able to speak again. "Well, wow. Um, can you tell him I'm not going anywhere with him and I would like him to return home to his own time period? *Now.*"

After looking up a few words, the professor translated, and the Viking's eyes shined with amusement as he answered.

The professor translated, "He's basically saying, no, you will come with him. And even if he was willing to leave you here, which he isn't, he won't go back with out you."

She shook her head. "Who do you think you are?" she asked the Viking directly. "You can't just step into my time and tell me to come to yours. I have a life here. And that wolf you were trying to fight earlier is the person I've chosen to spend the rest of my life with. Not you."

The professor had to look a few more words up in order to translate. But before he could even finish doing so the Viking was shaking his head and pounding his chest for emphasis.

"He says he will spray Rafe's blood across the snow for his insult—it's actually some pretty poetic stuff he's saying. Very

Beowulf-esque. But the main point is he wants you to know you are his."

"Can you explain to him in my time period, men don't own women? They don't drag them around by the hair, and he can't tell me what to do."

The professor flipped through the pages of his dictionary. "I can try."

"Good," she said, standing. "Exhibit number one can be me walking out of here to go be with the man I've chosen and love."

And she did just that, her own righteous anger fueling her steps.

But that anger faded when she found Rafe sitting on the clinic steps, hunched over with his fists balled up on top of his knees.

She dropped down beside him and strung her arm around his shoulders. "I'm sorry that happened," she whispered.

"Don't apologize," he said. But he leaned over toward her and Chloe was pretty certain he sniffed her for evidence of arousal before saying, "It's not your fault. This is some fucked up shit, but it's not your fault."

Her heart flooded with love for him then. And she nuzzled against his shoulder in the friendly way they used to before Rafe came into his manhood, before his brotherly affection became muddied with lust.

"I'll move in with you," she said.

He turned to her. "What?"

"I'll move in with you after the full moon. I want everyone, including your father, to know how much I love you and how committed I am to you and only you." She nudged him. "But you're going to have to get rid of that TV in the kitchen. I hate it."

He cupped her face in his warm hand. It was in the twenties that day, but wolves ran hot—male wolves even more so than female ones. "You just made me a very happy man."

"I want to be with you. I choose you," she told him.

"Well, I think you made the right choice," Rafe said, patting her knee. "Now, seriously, you want me to kill that chicken for you before I leave for work, right?"

Chloe let her head fall against her shoulder in embarrassment. "Right. I tried to do it myself this morning, but it looked at me with these big innocent eyes."

Rafe shook his head and chuckled.

"I know, I know," she said, before he could. "Worst wolf ever."

※

The day passed quickly with Chloe rushing to finish up her chicken and fennel recipe and get it edited and posted online before the full moon rose. Generally, Rafe bounced back from shifting with energy to spare, but turning into a wolf and then back into a human took a lot out of her. It often took up to forty-eight hours for her to sleep it off, and back when she'd been in school, almost all of her absences had been due to recovering from her monthly shift.

Rafe thought this was because she chose to cage herself up during full moon nights as opposed to running with the pack as he did. But as civilized as modern werewolves were in human form these days, they became particularly wild when they shifted, or "got wolf" as Rafe referred to it. They spent the entire night, in what seemed to Chloe to be a hunting-lust, taking out animals big and small, or whatever else crossed their paths.

A few times human hikers, who had ignored all the "No Trespassing" signs at the foot of Wolf Mountain, had gone missing or survived the attack and gotten changed into werewolves themselves. Back in the eighties, the number of wolf attacks had gotten so bad the North American Lupine Council had strictly forbidden shifting outside of full moon nights, just to keep the damages to a minimum.

In any case, it just wasn't in Chloe's nature to "get wolfed," so she chose to shift in the confines of her own home rather than running to the mountain with her fellow wolves.

About an hour before sunset, Doc Fischer called to tell her they'd made little to no progress in convincing the Viking to go back to his time. "He keeps telling the professor he can't go back without you. I'll cage him up before sunset, but we can't just keep him chained to a bed when he turns back into a human. I think it's time to bring the king in to handle this."

"Why do we have to bring the king into it?" she asked. "He can't make me go back in time with him."

"No he can't, that's why we're going to have to consult with him. We're at a stalemate, and he'll have to decide how to handle it."

Chloe rubbed a hand over her face. If anyone else were her mate, the king, who was an otherwise fair and level-headed leader, would side with the she-wolf. But since she was engaged to his son, he might just decide to declare their engagement null and void, if it meant freeing Rafe up to mate with another. The king liked her well enough, but he liked the king of Alaska's three daughters even better, and if he could forge an alliance and get grandpups, he'd probably be more than willing to kick Chloe to the curb.

Rafe had been right, if they had any hope of his father ruling in their favor, they had to make a strong show of commitment by moving in together.

"Or I could kill him," Rafe said when she called to give him the update. "That would solve everything."

"Rafe, you can't take a life. You may 'get wolf' one night a month, but you're still half-human and bound by council law."

"Yeah, yeah, yeah," Rafe muttered. "I'm just glad we're moving in together, even if it's under these circumstances."

"Me too," she lied, looking with real regret around her homey kitchen, which was pretty much the exact opposite of Rafe's uninviting and sterile one.

After she got off the phone, she started making her own preparations for the night's turn. Unlike Rafe, who simply met up with a bunch of his friends in the woods and stripped out of his clothes before shifting, her preparations were a bit more civilized. First, she plated up the rest of the chicken and fennel recipe and put it in the refrigerator. If she was lucky, it would be enough to tide her over for the next forty-eight hours. Next, she turned off all but a few lights and dug out a fresh pair of pajamas to wear the next day before descending the stairs into her basement. This was where her washing machine, dryer, and wolf cage lived.

The cage had come with the house. Wolves who didn't care to roam the countryside all night locked themselves in cages, so as to keep from destroying their homes as wolves were wont to do. Luckily for her, the house's last owner had felt as she had about turning outdoors and had installed a custom floor-to-ceiling cage.

When she moved in, she'd added the further amenity of covering the hard concrete floor with cushions made from the same soft but synthetic fabric used in chew-proof dog beds. She'd also placed her foster mother's record player outside the cage, so she'd have some form of entertainment while she waited for the turn. She usually spent her evenings crafting or reading, but she couldn't bring anything that she didn't want destroyed inside the cage, so that wasn't an option.

Listening to Myrna's old R&B records somehow made it feel like her foster mother was still alive and in her next-door cage, speaking soothing words to the pup Chloe had once been, while they both waited for the turn.

Myrna had possessed more heart than money, so she'd only been able to afford cramped dog cages for herself and the abandoned she-wolf pup she volunteered to care for. But still, Chloe had valued the fourteen years they had together, and liked to think back to those days when she curled up in her own cage, which was luxurious by comparison.

That night, she put the soundtrack to Mahogany on before closing herself into the cage and stripping down to her panties. She put the cage's key into the box on the far wall. Key boxes were another clever werewolf invention. They were placed just high enough so she couldn't get to it in wolf form, but could easily access it when she was human again and let herself out of her cage. This was another step up from the one Myrna had provided. Back then, they'd had to wait for Rafe's mother to come and let them out.

Rafe's mother had already told her she expected Chloe to take over the royal duty of opening the cages once she and Rafe were properly mated, and Chloe would be more than happy to do so. She liked that she'd be of true service once she became part of the royal Colorado family, and she was excited about her many upcoming duties. She just hoped the Viking didn't ruin everything for her.

With a sigh, she put the heavy cage key into the built-in box and laid down, covering herself up with the warm, indestructible fire blanket she kept in the cage for full moon nights. She then closed her eyes, listening to Diana Ross sing while she waited.

She soon dozed off and therefore didn't realize something was wrong until the music stopped playing, and the thunk of the needle slipping off the record jolted her awake.

She sat up, her eyes going to the basement window. But no, it was dark outside. Now that the music had stopped playing, she could even hear the far-off howls of her freshly-turned pack members. So why was she still in human form?

Her body began to tingle. At first she thought maybe it was the turn, come late, and she got to her knees, preparing to go feral. But the turn didn't happen, and the tingling continued, spreading over her still-human body until she was flush with fever, and sweating from the unrelenting prickling underneath her skin. It was as if all of her nerve endings had electricity coursing through them.

She must be sick, she thought. Usually wolf-sicknesses took the form of things like rabies, which contrary to her current situation, kept them in wolf form long after the sun had risen again. But maybe this was a wolf-sickness she had never heard of before.

She ran her hands over her face, which was flush but didn't seem to have anything wrong with it. She touched her neck next, checking her thyroid, but it seemed to be okay, too.

She ran her hands over her arms and legs, and even cupped her breast to give herself a self-examination. She'd never heard of a she-wolf contracting breast cancer, but since wolves weren't allowed to talk about being wolves on the internet, you never knew...

When her hand grazed her nipple, a sweet pain zapped through her, freezing her where she knelt and causing her to draw in her breath and then release it again with a short gasp. She looked down and saw that her nipples were now as hard as rocks. And as if they had minds of their own, her hands started kneading her breasts, her thumbs strumming over black-cherry-colored buds again and again, unable to stop themselves from exploring the sensations this action caused within her body.

Soon she felt a tugging sensation below, and the lips of her most intimate part clenched in and out in a wet silent beg, before it began to release something even she could now recognize as heat.

She was in heat, she realized foggily, literally dripping with the need to have a wolf mate with her. But Rafe was somewhere on the mountain, running through the night with his fellow pack members.

Chloe dimly recalled a Health class, in which they were informed that she-wolves in heat didn't turn, even during a full moon, nature's way of cutting down on possible birth defects.

No, once you went into heat, you stayed in heat until you were mated with a pup in your belly. And after that, neither you nor your mate turned again until three months after the baby's birth.

For the first time in her life, she touched her pussy for a reason other than cleaning it. The clenching was so insistent, the tentative rubbing against the swollen bulb between her folds proved to be too little. She was soon plunging her fingers into her tunnel, working them in and out, trying to find some relief.

But if anything, this only made it worse. As if angered by her meager offering, her pussy clenched even tighter, sucking her fingers into its vise grip, but refusing to be satiated by anything less than a mate's cock. Soon, tears of frustration began to roll down her cheeks. They weren't even an hour into the full moon and she wasn't sure how much longer she could bear the wait for Rafe to change back and come find her.

"Please, please…" she begged no one in particular as she rubbed herself against the mat, trying desperately to find some sort of release.

And that was when his scent filled her nostrils. She opened her teary eyes and found the Viking standing at the bottom of her stairs. He had clearly been watching her trying to masturbate. And his eyes were hot with one hundred percent unadulterated and extremely feral lust.

CHAPTER SEVEN

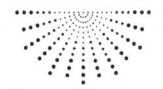

HIS captors locked him away in a cage, located in a below-ground room, the manner of which would have been impossible in his own land. They then walked away to heed the call of the moon.

Fenris had but one notion: to break out of his trap before he shifted. He took from around his neck a wolf medallion, which, when manipulated in the correct fashion, broke apart into two jagged pieces, one representing the wolf and one representing the man. Either half could be used as a false key, and thus did he release himself from his would-be jail. And he thought he beat the moon, but then he spied the full moon, sitting in the night sky, having already risen.

He stopped, narrowing his eyes at the sight. Did the wolves of this land have potions that interrupted the shift? The tutor they had beckoned to translate his tongue had told him the fated mates spell had moved him over a thousand years into the future. He had heard tales of the spell transporting wolves through not just space, but also time. But just as he had never met anyone in the flesh who had travelled to and from Valhalla, he had never met anyone who had traveled through time as it was claimed the spell could do.

Until now.

What strange land had the spell delivered him to? The moon had driven its chariot into the sky. Yet he remained a man. He waited, all the while, feeling the moon coursing through his body, but nothing happened.

That is, nothing happened until the smell of his mate's arousal reached his nostrils, strong and as thick as the smoke from a pit fire. And then did he understand why he had yet to shift.

His fated mate was in heat.

Now not just the moon, but also her mating call burned in his blood. 'Twas fortunate for him the medicine man had left his pants and sword to lie in the front room of the building, or else he would not have had the presence of mind to grab them both as he followed her smell out of the entrance.

His nose led him to a cabin made of wood, less than half a *rast* from the place he had been kept. However, after he let himself in, though he could smell her everywhere, he could find her nowhere on the premises. Finally, he threw open a door that led into another below-ground room, much like the one he had been placed in himself.

And when he reached the bottom of the steps, he found his beautiful mate, writhing on a floor matted with black cushions, her hand moving in an out of her womanhood, her face twisted in the pain of sexual need.

Fenris had not thought it possible to be more aroused than he had been with the scent of his fated mate's heat in his nose, but seeing her like this made his manhood jump and swell further to the point of pain, to the point that he could not be certain he could take her without going beserk in the way of a warrior in a blood-frenzy on the battlefield.

He breathed deep, seeking the warrior's control over his wolf, even as it growled to be mated with the she-wolf he had crossed time to retrieve.

She stopped with a gasp, removing her hand from her puss, and staring at him in horror. A moment of shocked quiet, and then she began to shake her head back and forth, speaking her strange language, so rapidly he doubted he could have understood her even if he spoke her tongue.

It made little matter, though. The time for words had come and gone. He went to the cage and jerked at the door, only to find it locked.

He rattled it, expecting the wide-eyed she-wolf to bid him entry. But she merely stood there, shaking her head, even as he could see her heat, dripping from her womanhood, all but begging him enter.

He shook the cage door and demanded, "Open this door."

But she backed into the corner, as far out of his reach as possible. Cursing, he once again untied the cord around his neck. He worked the lock with a hunter's focus until the door swung open, finally allowing him entrance.

His she-wolf scrambled, talking loudly at him in her language, words he did not understand but could comprehend despite not knowing her tongue.

"You deny your need for me?"

She shook her head and said many more words, only one of which he recognized. "Rafe."

"You would speak his name to me when I am your fated mate," he snarled.

She looked up at the ceiling and then back at him, conveying through body language that she was exasperated before speaking more words.

"No," he declared, cutting her off. "I am your fated mate. I would have us join now without delay and then return to my own land, once I have planted my seed within your belly."

But when he made to step to her, she scrambled away from

him, darting toward the open door in a move that so surprised him, she almost managed to escape.

However, his warrior's reflexes did not fail him. He caught her by the waist just as she got one foot through the door and in two more moves, he had her on the floor, pinned beneath him.

A wolf with less control would have taken her right there, protests be damned. But his fated mate looked up at him with such fear in her eyes, it gave him pause. He bit back against his own need, shoving it down as if it were some little thing and not the beginning of the mating frenzy he knew it to be.

"Shhh," he said, making the same soothing sound he used to calm his horse when she became agitated. "I will not hurt you, and I would not have you fear our mating."

She gasped out a few more words, and he felt her arms moving between them, struggling to break free. But eventually she stopped squirming beneath him, and then she lie there, breathing hard.

Fenris smoothed a hand over her hair, waiting with a patience he did not feel for her to calm herself. And even when her breathing slowed to a regular pace, he continued to lie there, allowing the fear to fully evaporate, so she, too, could come to understand the obvious.

They were the only two un-shifted wolves in the village, they were fated mates, and they would be consummating their union before the sun dragged her chariot across the sky.

❄

Less than seventy-two hours ago, Chloe didn't think things could possibly get any more awkward. She was a twenty-five year old virgin she-wolf who could barely stand to kiss her alpha prince fiancé, because she hadn't gone into heat. Then a time-traveling Viking showed up to claim her as his fated mate. She had begun to think surely her life couldn't possibly get more messed up than that.

And then she had unexpectedly gone into heat and been found attempting to masturbate her way to relief by the Viking she was currently trying to convince to go back to his own time period without her.

At that moment, there was really nothing left to do except get angry. "*C'mon*! Cut a she-wolf a break, why don't you?" she said to the Viking. "Are you seriously here? Are you seriously, *seriously* here in my basement?"

But her anger was soon replaced with fear when the Viking advanced on the cage.

"No-no-no-no-no!" she said holding up her hand in the universal sign for stop. "Do not come near me. I am not letting you in here, so you can just get that idea out of your head right freaking now."

He throttled the bars and said something in his language she was sure translated to, "Let me in, woman."

She scrambled to the back of the cage, pressing herself flat against the basement's brick wall and willing it to absorb her. Her nether regions were still throbbing with need, but her mind knew she had to wait for Rafe to shift back into a human and come claim her.

What was the Viking doing un-shifted anyway? And out of the clinic's cage, which doubled as their town's jail, and which Doc Fischer had assured her he'd be put in before the moon set?

She soon had the answer to the second question, when he untied the medallion from around his neck and used it to let himself into the cage she'd hope would keep her protected from him.

The fear inside her gut doubled in size and though she knew it was a long shot, she ran for the door, hoping to get upstairs fast enough to lock him in the basement, which had a deadbolt that wouldn't be easily surmounted by a necklace.

But just as she made it to the cage entrance, he grabbed her by the arm and the next thing she knew, she was pinned underneath him. Man, he was fast for a big guy.

"No!" she cried. "I don't care what time period you're from, I'm not going to let you rape me." She fought to free her hands from between their bodies, so she could go for his eyes. But he adjusted himself, somehow redistributing his weight so she not only couldn't free her hands, but also couldn't squirm any part of her body, except the one screaming at her to let him fuck her. Right now.

She looked up and away from him, refusing to meet his eyes as he forced himself on her. But...

...nothing happened. In fact, the next thing she felt was his hand, smoothing back her hair. His breath was hot on her face, but calm, not the ragged affair of someone about to do his worst to a woman.

Her eyes slowly lowered to meet his, and she found him gazing back at her, his own gray eyes soft with infinite patience, as if he had all the time in the world to wait her out.

She felt her heartbeat slowing down as she got lost in that gray gaze of his, and soon she became uncomfortably aware of the large piece of male anatomy pressed against her folds. She could feel its heat, even through the cloth of his basketball shorts. Her own heat called out in answer with an urgency that scared her even more than the idea of possibly being forced to mate with him against her will.

"No, no, no, please," she whispered, trying to hold on to thoughts of her fiancé, but her body seemed to have a mind of its own and she could feel her hips begin to move against his as if divorced from her better nature.

And maybe she could have gotten herself under control, forced her body to stay still beneath his despite her state of arousal, but when he covered her mouth with his again, her last shred of decency flew away into the night.

This kiss felt like coming home, like water on a hot day, like bread fresh from the oven, the start of a perfect meal. She undulated underneath him, and he made a harsh sound, his Old Norse now coming out hard and fast. He lifted up his chest enough to allow her the use of her hands, which she laced into his long hair, pulling him down for more of his drug-like kisses.

But soon the kisses grew to be too little. She needed him inside her. It hurt so bad that he wasn't already there, something deep inside her ached in such a painfully sweet way that she soon found herself begging for what she had tried to escape just a few minutes ago.

"Please, please mate with me," she said now, hating herself for her loss of control, but feeling she would die if he didn't—

He pushed inside of her with no warning, except for the feel of his hands gripping her sides as he did so. And she cried out against the arc of red-hot pain that shot through her core as he tore through the barrier protecting her virginity.

He kissed her several times as if to mitigate the pain, saying something in Old Norse between each one, and she found herself feeling grateful for his kisses. They distracted her from the pain below, which soon began to fade.

His eyes drifted down to her breasts, and he bent his head to kiss one, lathing her nipple with his tongue. He then sucked on it so hard, she could feel a corresponding tug below, as her legs came up to fold around his waist, for reasons she didn't quite get until she felt him sink into her even deeper.

They both groaned as he thrust into her again and again, his hard body rolling into the cradle of her thighs. She held on to his forearms, her own hips involuntarily moving into his, seeking relief from the sweet fire burning in her womb. "I need, I need, I need…" she said, not quite able to put a label on it.

He captured her lips with his again, and rocked into her with a long, slow thrust, causing her to moan when the rub of his chest shot twin bolts of electric pleasure through her nipples.

Every single inch of her felt swollen with desire, but also tight with need. She couldn't stop herself from mating with this man, even though he was more or less a stranger to her. When she tried to consider pulling away from her, her body went crazy in protest, thrusting her hips into his even harder as if to punish her for even thinking such a thing.

But then he pulled out himself.

"No!" she cried.

But he made the same sound he used to quiet her down before. At the same time, he easily flipped her on to her stomach, and she barely had time to scramble to her knees, before he was on her again. This time ramming into her from behind in what she recognized as the most primal of mating rituals.

The man, she realized, had taken her virginity in missionary, so as to lessen the pain of her breaching. But the wolf inside of him would settle for nothing less than a full mounting. All softness disappeared from him then as he fell over her back, his thick erection sliding in and out of her as he grunted above her.

Whatever shred of humanity had allowed him to take her gently before was gone now, and for Chloe, who couldn't move beneath his heavy body, it felt like being claimed by some sort of flesh-covered beast.

Their sex had taken such an intense turn, she should have been scared out of her mind, but something primal in her responded to this position. She could feel the mating knot now at the base of his penis, hard and unforgiving, and pressed against her G-spot in ways that made it impossible to regret what she was doing. She actually felt the inside of her vagina swell around his wolf knot, keeping him locked in place as he rutted her.

And then came the thing she hadn't quite known she'd been waiting for…her eyes rolled and her breath caught in her throat as wave after wave of the most intense pleasure she had ever known slammed into her. Then she was breathing again, but he was still moving into her, one large calloused hand covering her breast as his thrusts became faster and faster. And to her astonishment another orgasm began to overtake her.

White noise filled her head and in the distance, she could hear somebody screaming. Only when the orgasm began to fade away did she realize it was her.

Her arms collapsed underneath her and she fell to her elbows, unable to hold herself up anymore. Everything on her body felt like quivering jelly, but despite this, her pussy kept clenching around his cock, milking it with hungry wantonness, her wolf not caring who this Viking was or what promises she had made to another.

And when she felt the hot stream of cum begin to release inside of her, another orgasm began to overtake her, this one ripping through every part of her body as his seed flooded into her hot and strong, spilling into her womb and sending her human over the edge. She screamed and cried, babbling nonsensical words until finally the vise of pleasure began to ebb away, and there was nothing left but her and the Viking on the matted floor of the cage.

His face was now pressed into the back of her neck and he was making that soothing sound again. "Shhh," he said. "It is done. We are mated."

She trembled underneath him, but she felt her heartbeat once again slowing down as she came back from whatever wild place the mating had sent her. "That was so..." She didn't have the words.

"Yea, for me, as well." With more gentleness than she would think a man his size could possess, he arranged their bodies, so they were lying on their sides, with him behind her, still embedded inside her swollen folds.

Every wolf knew what happened on heat night, that it was called such because after the mating, the wolf and his mate, stayed physically locked in this most intimate embrace "into the night" or thirty to sixty minutes, if you were being completely technical. But still, it was slightly embarrassing to feel herself involuntarily clenching around his thick unit, refusing to let it go until it had milked every drop of cum from him.

As if reading her thoughts, he rested his hand over her still-swollen breasts. "There is no need to feel embarrassment. You availed yourself well this night, and I am well-pleased."

Something prickled inside of her. "Your pleasure wasn't my main point of concern."

"Yet, have you achieved it. You should be happy to have so pleased your mate." He chuckled and thrust into her in a low-grade, teasing way. Nonetheless it sent a lovely wave of afterglow through her, which indeed, made her forget her embarrassment about holding a man she barely knew in the vise grip of her vagina.

"We will sleep now. We mayhap have many days of mating ahead of us before we are able to make travel back to the gate," he told her, with a squeeze of her breast. "By Fenrir, even though I am a king, I find it hard to believe such beauty belongs to me. My fellow wolves will envy me this treasure."

She had every intention of letting him know she still had no intention of traveling back in time with him and would never meet his fellow wolves because she would be staying in her own time, thank you very much. But sleep was already dragging her down, so hard she could barely form thoughts, much less words.

In fact, she didn't even notice she was talking to him, even though she hadn't moved her mouth, or that she could now understand every word he said, until right before the blackness enveloped her.

CHAPTER EIGHT

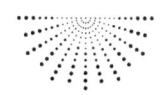

CHLOE woke up feeling like she had been run over by a school bus. But she also woke up alone. She sat up on the cage's matted floor and looked around. She was definitely alone. And the smell of her own heat was so thick in the air, it obscured anything else that might have been there before.

Maybe, she thought, it had all been a dream. Maybe she had gone into heat and gone crazy with arousal, conjuring up the Viking who was in actuality still locked in the clinic's cage. But when she got to her feet she had plenty evidence of what had happened in the throbbing raw and used feeling between her legs.

And if that wasn't enough to tip her off that last night had really happened, her wolf ears picked up the sound of someone moving around upstairs. With a sigh, she walked over to the pajamas she'd laid out the night before. She was momentarily frozen in place by guilt however, when she saw that this particular set was covered in white horses with orange manes. The Broncos pajamas had been a Christmas gift from Rafe's father the year before, and she'd worn them every morning following a full moon since.

Where was Rafe now? It was only a matter time before he found out...

Chloe pushed those thoughts out of her head and pulled on the pajamas. She couldn't think about that now. She was starving, her body felt like one huge sexualized nerve ending, and she had a Viking stomping around her house. She'd deal with the consequences of betraying her fiancé later. Right now she needed food.

She found the Viking standing stark naked in the kitchen, turning the knob on her stove back and forth, his face crinkled in confusion as the flames switched on and off.

As unhappy about this situation as she was, for a few seconds she became mesmerized by the sight of his rock-hard body, which didn't look like it was carrying even an ounce of extra flesh on it.

But then she cleared her mind with a shake of her head and asked him telepathically, "What are you doing?"

"This flame doth appear with the turn of a dial. 'Tis magic?" he asked, continuing to turn the flame on and off.

"First of all, please stop." She came to stand beside him, but stopped just short of touching him, which she sensed would be dangerous in the state her body was in. "You are literally playing with fire. Second of all, no, it's not magic."

"Then how is such possible?"

"Well there's gas and there's this thing called a pilot light." She struggled to come up with an explanation for how her gas stove worked, but realized she didn't quite know herself. "It's hard to explain, because the thing about now as opposed to your time is we have a lot of technology we use, but most people couldn't even begin to tell you how it works."

"So then this 'technology'—this is how you call your magic? The kind of which my own aunt, who is a sorceress, might perform?"

"Sort of. But instead of sorceresses we have engineers. They understand how these things work, but nobody else does. The truth is we don't really care as long as we can cook our food."

"Things are much the same way in my own time. Most do not care to learn spells or perform rituals themselves, only benefit from them. Still, your engineer-sorceresses must be very powerful indeed if they are able to create dial-heat and also invisible heat for your home."

"Yes, I suppose they are," she said. "But speaking of magic, how is it we can suddenly understand each other? When did you start speaking English?"

He gave her a confused look. "I would ask the same of you. I thought you were speaking Norse to me. A strange version of it, yea, but a Norse which can be understood by my ears."

"No," she said. "I'm definitely not speaking Norse. And I guess that means you're not speaking English."

"Nay. It would seem our being fated mates would serve as a translator."

She narrowed her eyes. "You're saying our ability to use telepathy is allowing us to talk back and forth despite our language barrier."

"Telepathy—this be Greek for talk of the mind's eye, yea?"

"Yes," she answered.

"Then yea, that be my conclusion." He patted the stove, as if that subject were thoroughly closed. "Now, you may prepare us a feast so we may break our fast before we mate again."

"Um, excuse me?" she said.

He crooked his head to the side and his eyes hooded. "I can smell the strength of your arousal. You would have me again, and I would have you."

"Yeah, but…" Her throat went dry and her cheeks heated with embarrassment. Did he have to point out he could smell her?

"Are you not trained in the woman's arts?" he asked. "Have your engineers come up with…" He paused to remember the word. "…'technology' by which food may be prepared for you?"

And that was how Chloe Adams, the woman behind one of the most popular do-it-yourself blogs in the United States, ended up fixing the werewolf who had crossed time and space to get to her a year-old frozen dinner as his first meal in her home.

Fenris was fascinated by the "technology magic" of the microwave and that it "emitted no heat outside of its cage."

But he was confused by the meal itself. "It tastes good, but it does ring false on tongue," he said, frowning.

Chloe, who was at the stove, fixing herself an egg scramble and doggedly ignoring the fact that she could feel her heat dripping into panties, answered, "That's the preservatives you're tasting, all the chemicals they use to make the food keep for a long time. But don't worry."

She pushed the egg scramble onto a plate, which she set in front of him. "You'll like this better. It's made with all organic ingredients."

He shifted his fork away from the frozen dinner and dug into the scramble. After the first bite, he nodded, grinning as he chewed. "I should not have accused you of being untrained in the woman's arts. Your skill does please my stomach greatly."

Chloe glowed a bit under the compliment. "Thanks."

He scooted back in his chair and patted his lap. "I would have you share this meal with me."

Even after what they'd done last night, Chloe could not help but feel awkward with this request. Yes, they were mated now, but that didn't eclipse the fact that she still barely knew him, and she was still riddled with guilt about Rafe...

"Actually, I can make another one for myself. Scrambles are really easy. Too easy, really. I usually put in more effort than this, especially with guests. I'm a little embarrassed, actually—"

She cut off mid-ramble when his hand snaked around her wrist.

"I would have us share," he repeated.

Before she could deny his request a second time, she found

herself tumbling down into his lap, her back landing against his hard chest, her butt firmly nestled into his erection.

He ate half of the scramble with his arm anchored around her waist, then he handed her the fork and watched her finish off the rest in a silence that almost seemed to crackle with sexual tension. It was all she could do to keep herself still on his lap as she finished their shared breakfast.

"Tell me," he said after she took her last bite. "Why have you so much looking glass on your cooking room wall?"

It took her a moment to realize he was talking about the kitchen wall, which was lined in mirrored tile. "Oh, um, well, it's kind of hard to explain. What you call the woman's arts—that's kind of what I do for a living."

"A living?" he asked, confusion in his voice.

"That's my job. Do you know job?"

"Yea, I see, you cook for others. As a servant."

"Yes, but not really for others, and definitely not as a servant. Basically, I make up recipes and crafts then I show other people how to do them. For example, this bender chair we're sitting in. I made that out of peachleaf willow, mainly for the purpose of showing other people how to make the same thing."

"You are a tutor then? Like the man who did translate my tongue for you before."

"Um, sort of. It's more like what I guess you'd call theater. I perform cooking and crafting in front of other people and they watch me do it. And I use the mirror to make sure what I'm doing looks correct."

"The woman's arts are considered entertainment in this time?"

"Yeah. Cooking and making things yourself are more like hobbies and less like needed skills these days."

"I am intrigued by your job," he informed her. "And we shall speak more of it, but for now I think we must leave this topic. Your need has grown too great for further conversation."

She wanted to deny his assessment of her need, except it was one hundred percent accurate. She was almost pitifully grateful when his hands found the front of her pajama top and ripped it open, sending the buttons flying across the room.

Her pajama bottoms came off next, followed by her panties, which fully unleashed the smell of her extreme arousal into the air and sent them both into a frenzy.

This wasn't anything like the candlelit affair she'd imagined when Rafe first proposed. No, in this reality, the Viking yanked her braid to arch her head back and growled in her ear. "Watch me claim you in your wall of looking glass."

And she couldn't help but do just that, watching the contrast of their skin, his pale, hers dark, as he lifted her up in his lap and pushed into her wet heat. He then cupped both her breasts in his large hands and leaned back in the chair with her, before proceeding to move into her from behind, his thrusts long and deep.

To have him inside her like this felt like nothing short of heaven to Chloe. The wolf knot at the base of his penis once again found its way to the special erogenous zone inside her pussy and lodged against it, again and again, making her moan with every stimulating stroke. But there was something missing, something she couldn't quite put her finger on, until one of his hands descended from her breast, and he put two of his large fingers on the bundle of nerves at the front of her entrance."

"Oh!" She bucked against him, her body unconsciously attempting to unseat itself, even as her mind called out for more. The only thing that kept her from completely losing it on top of him was the Viking's strong hand cupping her in front and keeping her firmly pinned to his cock. "What are you doing? I've never felt anything so…"

He provided no answer to her question, merely drank in the sight of them in the mirror together as he relentlessly plundered her depths. "Watch us together, beauty. See how I claim you."

And for a moment, she, too, became enthralled by the erotic sight of herself spread out so wantonly on the Viking's lap, her back arched in pleasure, a look of sex-crazed abandon on her face, as each stroke sent her closer to the edge...

Before she finally fell over it with a long scream, and she had to close her eyes as the climax overtook her. Perhaps the sight of her coming so hard in the mirror sent him over the edge as well. He soon yelled out his own pleasure, and she felt the rush of his seed inside of her.

His forehead fell against her back. "You are my undoing, beauty."

As if in answer, she felt the powerful clenching of her own vagina around his wolf's knot as it continued to hungrily milk his dick.

His hands once again found her breasts. "Upon the next mating, I must put a mind to comfort. I cannot allow you to make me so mad with lust that we end up locked together in a chair."

Chloe groaned in agreement. "Seriously, how are we going to get out of sitting like this for the next hour?"

Somehow they figured it out, negotiating themselves onto the kitchen's braided area rug before all but passing out again. The mating frenzy, she was beginning to discover, took a lot out of both of its occupants.

CHAPTER NINE

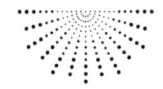

WHEN Chloe woke up a few hours later, having apparently released Fenris while they slept, she was beyond ravenous. Still, after she stood up, she took a few moments to ogle the Viking's sleeping form. He lie on his side, his left arm still slung across the space she had recently abandoned. And his cock didn't seem to be getting any rest at all. It was fully erect, the mushroom at its head looking particularly hard and swollen now that his wolf's knot was hidden away.

She once again felt her own breasts swell and the previously low-grade fire of her heat kicked up a notch, making it so she had to turn away from him if she wanted to stay in control.

She ended up putting a plate of the chicken and fennel in her microwave, which she rarely used, preferring to heat her meals back up either in or on top of the stove. But she was in a rush to feed her human before her wolf took back over, so she made an exception.

Afterwards she took a quick shower, and slipped on the silk kimono robe she'd made for a special Asian-American History Month episode of Black Mountain Woman. She then started to fill the tub for the Viking. She wasn't sure he'd be able to work a shower, and maybe he could manage to get a bath in before they got trapped in another mating frenzy.

"What manner of magic is this that you would be able to fill a tub of this size by yourself and in so little time?" a deep voice asked.

She nearly jumped out of her skin before turning to see Fenris standing behind her, still stark naked, and not seeming to be the least bit embarrassed about it.

"Did I frighten you?"

"Yeah, sorry, I'm not really used to having men in my home."

He gave her a thoughtful look. "In my time, a maiden would not live on her own as you do. Where is your family?"

A pang went off in her heart, thinking about the parents who had abandoned her, and the Nightwolf family she'd been hoping to join.

"This you do not wish to talk about?" he guessed.

"No, not really," she answered.

He gave her another long, considering look before saying, "Then tell me of your magic bath vessel."

"Well, we have these things called pipes," she answered, "Kind of like the Roman aqueduct system, but with hot and cold running water pushed through these metal tube thingies."

He gave a sage nod. "Your engineers are powerful sorceresses indeed."

"Indeed," she agreed. She stood up and pointed at the bar of soap in the built-in dish below the shower head. "There's the soap. I've got to get back to the kitchen to warm up a plate of food for you. But just holler if you need anything."

"I shall 'holler' now," he answered, capturing her hands and placing them on his bare chest. "I have need of grooming."

"Oh, you mean like a shave?" Chloe's eyes lit up. "Are you serious, because I found this old-fashioned straight razor at a flea market that I've been dying to try out for an episode of my show, but—" She cut herself off before saying Rafe wouldn't let her test it out on him. Instead she finished with, "—but I haven't had the chance to use it yet."

"In my time, it is the she-wolf who decides the grooming of her mate. If you would have me bare of face as the men in your land, I shall not argue."

Chloe could see he was a little reluctant to part with his beard, but she was dying to see what he looked like under all that facial hair, so she didn't do the polite thing and offer to just give him a trim. "Awesome. Just sit right here on the counter."

Forty minutes, one towel wrapped around the Viking's waist, and a few bumbling explanations about how a video camera worked, later, Chloe scraped away the last of the shaving cream to reveal what turned out to be a man with movie star good looks, complete with a square jaw and a strong chin that when paired with his intense grey eyes, somehow made him look even more bad-ass than he had with a sword.

"Wow, you're really good-looking," she told him.

"'Tis a surprise, I see," he said, with a teasing smile.

"No, I just didn't expect the face to match the body."

He took the razor out of her hand and set it aside on the counter before, once again, taking her hands in his and placing them on his chest. From what Chloe could tell, this seemed to be his favorite talking position, at least where she was concerned.

"I am glad you are well-pleased with my face as I am with yours."

He then began to lean his face towards hers.

"Nuh-uh-uh," she said, averting her lips. "I've still got to warm up your food and figure out how to wash your leather pants, and we've got to re-run your bath."

"Do not hie away," he said, rubbing his nose into the side of the face she turned away from him. "I wish to gaze upon you as I soap, and I would also have you wash my hair."

She laughed. "I think you can handle washing your own hair."

"Your skin is very soft. I find it hard to believe you have really passed twenty and five summers as you claim."

"Well, we have this stuff called moisturizing lotion these days. It's kind of like a liquid butter for your face. And it helps our skin stay softer longer—"

He took a hold of her chin and turned her face back towards him, cutting off her explanation with a firm kiss. "Your lips are also soft. Is this to be credited to your liquid butter as well?" he asked, before running his own lips down her neck.

"No, the stuff I use on my lips is more like an ointment," she said, trying to stay firm in her resolve, even though his kisses had her heat smell filling up the small room. "I really should go."

"And these?" he asked, reaching into her robe and palming her breasts with both hands. "What manner of butter do you use to keep them so soft?"

She bit her lip against the sweet, aching tug his playing with her breast induced. "Fenris, seriously, you need to stop."

He untied her robe. "You are softer all over than any woman I have ever known. Mayhap even down here." He cupped her mound, pressing the ball of his palm into her clit.

"Yea," he said, his voice a deep whisper. "Most assuredly softer."

And that's how she ended up sleeping off their third mating in a drained bathtub, waiting for them to unlock.

This time when she woke up, she was starving and she knew Fenris would be too, considering he'd only had breakfast. She left him in the bathtub. Even with her extra werewolf strength, she doubted she'd be able to move someone as large as him by herself. Plus, she was finding out the hard way that when sexual heat was involved, they had a rather narrow window of time between both of them being awake and frenzied boom-chicca-wow-wow.

First she consulted the internet about how to clean his leather pants and spent half an hour gently rubbing the soft suede with white vinegar and a dry cloth. Then she tried to clean his ridiculously heavy sword, partly to be nice, but mostly because who wanted a sword coated with animal blood lying around the house? But she figured out why neither the doctor nor the professor had tried to clean the sword themselves, when her fingers came away burning, the cleaning cloth she had attempted to use on it ruined by hers body's reaction to the blade. Apparently Fenris did not mess around when it came to getting his sword fight on. The entire blade was covered in silver. So she ended up lining the tub in the guest bathroom with aluminum foil and using baking soda, boiling water, a wooden stick, and a rag to clean the blade without burning her fingers off.

By the time she was finished she had worked up a nice appetite, so she heated up the last two plates of chicken and fennel, but frowned when she set them on the counter. She doubted this would be enough food for both her and the six foot-something werewolf who hadn't eaten all day. And she cursed herself for not having any easy-to-make packaged food in the house, other than the one emergency microwave dinner, which was already gone.

Technically, she didn't "believe" in food that wasn't made completely from scratch, and on the rare occasion she didn't feel like cooking, she either went out to eat or ordered a pizza.

But she wasn't sure a pizza would get here in time for her to not succumb to another mating with the Viking. And even if she did call, she doubted the local pizzeria, which was owned by one of Rafe's high school basketball teammates, would be willing to deliver.

Thinking of the other Wolf Springs residents, who were all shifted back to humans and probably fully aware of what had happened between her and the Viking by now, sent another wave of guilt through her body.

Usually, when a female went into heat and joined with her mate, the town pitched in to keep them fed. She herself had left too many stews and pasta dishes to count outside of doorways, dreaming of the day when it would be her official job to either carry out or organize others to do this duty as Rafe's mate.

But no one had approached the house, much less left food. No one would dare cross the alpha prince in that manner, even the wolves she had left food for when they'd gone into heat.

She frowned to herself. There was nothing to be done but throw on some real clothes and make a trip out to her chicken house.

A few minutes later, she was overjoyed to find a veritable feast of eight whole eggs. That meant she wouldn't have to work up the guts to wring a chicken's neck for the first time by herself until the following day.

The find filled her with an unexplainable relief and for a moment, her guilt and anxiety slipped away. Maybe, just maybe, everything would be all right, she thought, putting the eggs in her basket.

Then she emerged from the chicken house and found her ex-fiancé standing in her backyard, his hair a ragged mess, and an axe in his right hand.

CHAPTER TEN

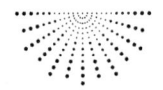

"RAFE," she whispered, going very still. "Put the axe down. Please."

He looked down at the menacing tool as if just now noticing it. "I'm not going to hurt you with this. I'm giving it back to you. Remember, I borrowed it from you last month." His eyes came back up to glare at her. "But I'm glad your opinion of me is so low now that you think I'd hurt a defenseless woman. Even one who betrayed me like you have."

"I'm sorry, Rafe," she said, clutching the basket of eggs to her chest. "It's been really crazy, and I didn't expect to see you so soon."

He leaned the axe against the tree stump she used to split logs. "Yeah well, you wouldn't have seen me at all if you hadn't decided to come out to your hen house at the same time I decided to return your axe."

She looked down at her eggs. "Yeah, well, I wouldn't have come out to the hen house if somebody had left us some food. The age-old tradition of helping your fellow wolf seems to have fallen by the way side since last night's moon."

His gaze went angry and cold. "Maybe they're too embarrassed for you. Everybody heard you screaming last night, and this morning, and then again a couple of hours ago. You could barely bring yourself to kiss me, but apparently all you want to do with him is fuck." He sneered. "If I'd known you had that in you, I might have taken you up on your offer to fuck me before your heat night. You know, the one you made less than forty-eight hours ago?"

Shame curdled her insides. "I'm sorry, Rafe. I don't have the words to tell you how sorry I am." She took a step toward him. "As cliché as this sounds, I never meant to hurt you. And I was telling the truth when I said you were my best friend. If he hadn't been there when I went into heat—"

He cut her off with a rough shake of his head. "I don't want to hear what happened or any of your excuses. I don't give a damn anymore, Chloe. We are definitely no longer friends. In fact, my new number one goal in life is to try to forget I was ever stupid enough to fall in love with you."

He looked so hurt that Chloe felt torn between begging him to forgive her and comforting him as she always did when he got angry. In the end, she reached out and took him into her arms, hugging him as tightly as she could. "I'm sorry. I'd give anything not to have hurt you this way."

For a moment his arms wrapped around her, too, and he hugged her back, just as tight. But then he said, "I can smell your heat—and his fucking scent all over you." Rafe's voice cracked, and that broke her, too.

She cried into his shoulder for what they'd lost, for what they could have been if Rafe had been there when she went into heat and not the Viking.

But he only let the embrace go on for a little while before pulling away from her. "I'm leaving town for a few weeks. I'm going to spend spring with my family in Alaska."

By "family in Alaska," he meant the king of Alaska. His father's best friend was the alpha of Alaska. And though Rafe wasn't actually related by blood to the king or his three daughters, they'd spent so many summers in each other homes that they referred to each other as family.

She almost told him to say hi to Alisha, her favorite of the Alaska alpha's three daughters, but then she remembered what Rafe had said about them no longer being friends. Said and probably meant.

As if reading her thoughts, he said, "I want you both gone when I get back. Especially him. If he's still here, I swear to God, I will ghost him, I don't care what it fucking takes."

Her eyes widened in alarm. "First of all, you're not the alpha yet, and even if you were, you couldn't just banish me. Second of all, where am I supposed to go if I don't live in Wolf Springs? This is my home, the only one I've ever known."

"Actually, it's my home. I own the mortgage, and I never charged you rent. So you have no rights when it comes to this place," he reminded her. "You can either move to another wolf town or go back to wherever the Viking came from. I don't care what you do. I never want to see you again."

"Rafe—"

He turned around and began walking away from her without another word.

"Rafe," she called after him again.

But he just left without ever once looking back at her. She knew he didn't, because she watched him walk away, until he disappeared into the distance.

❇

*F*enris woke up hungry and cold and slightly sore from having passed much time in a bathing tub. Yet, his body immediately craved his fated mate again. More than food, more than warmth, more than any comfort that sleeping on top of a true bed might afford him.

As a wolf of twenty and seven winters, he had seen many of his fellow pack members go into a mating frenzy with a she-wolf in heat, but of course he had never experienced it for himself.

Though the scent of a female's heat arousal had intrigued him, it had never sent him over the edge as it did with some wolves, causing good friends to turn on each other and attack the other with battle axes, if it meant claiming the she-wolf they desired.

But the lot of a fated mate seemed to be even worse. He had been more than ready to kill the man who dared to kiss his dark beauty even before they mated. Now the mere thought of that other wolf touching what was his made him want to learn one of his aunt's darker spells so he might run the man through with his sword, bring him back to life, then so end him again. Morbid thoughts, indeed. And not ones befitting a Fenris.

Fenris alphas did not get into fights over she-wolves. They were Fenris alphas, which meant such was never necessary. Any she-wolf in heat living on his lands would gladly have him as her mate if he would claim her. Indeed, another alpha king in his position would have simply chosen the most beautiful maiden in his village, spoken her name as his for her heat night, and put a pup in her belly.

But Fenris had been too occupied with the setting right of his kingdom in the wake of his father's rule that he had not cared to bother with such things. There had been alliances to re-forge, enemies to push back, hurt egos to soothe with riches, which he had been pressed to seek out himself since his father had done little to replenish their coffers during his last days as king.

In truth, the travails of rebuilding their kingdom had made the thought of mating, especially a fated mating, distasteful to Fenris. If he had been left to his own devices, he might not have bothered with the matter for another five to ten winters.

However, his Chloe made him wish he had uttered the words of the incantation that much sooner. Had ever there been a more exotic beauty? Buxom, quick of mind, well-skilled in the woman's arts, with an instinct toward losti even though she had never been touched before he. She made him want to dally in their mating frenzy, even if it meant not returning to his own lands forthwith.

And that, he thought, heaving himself out of her white tub, bothered him much. At no other time had he ever thought to put a she-wolf before his own interests. He had often derided both his allies and his enemies for doing so, and he had never been able to fathom finding himself in such place, of wanting to spend more time with his mate for purposes other than putting a babe in her belly. He feared he was already becoming as bewitched by the she-wolf called Chloe as his own father had been bewitched by his own fated mate.

Even more so, when he entered the kitchen, and found not only a delicious meal of chicken and fennel waiting for him, but also his leather pants, freshly laundered and his The King Maker, gleaming under the flameless lights, looking as new as the day he had laid down much coin for it. He smiled to himself, thinking of how his chieftains would envy him this she-wolf who cared not for the magics of her own time but had tutored herself in the arts of his, as if she had some heed she would one day be his alpha queen.

At that moment, he spied her in the kitchen window, standing in the yard behind her house, staring off into the distance with a basket of eggs gripped tight in one hand. He could not help but admire her lovely visage, framed as she was by the setting sun and clothed as she was in the same sort of dress and short wool coat she had worn when they first met outside the gate on the mountain. The dress was frilly on top and edged with lace. It put him in mind of the smocks that she-wolves wore in his own time, mostly under other clothes, but also by themselves in the warmth of the summer. It made her look like she belonged more in his time than her own. Watching her then, he understood the draw of fated mates, why young she-wolves followed his aunt around like puppies, begging her for the spell.

He now rued the time they had spent apart as he felt his heart, which had become icy with cynicism during his reign as king, begin to thaw. And within his mind grew a notion to join her outside and take her against a tree, so as to have the sun set on their fourth joining.

But then she suddenly turned back toward the house. This is when he saw her pass the side of her hand under one eye and then the other.

She had been crying, he realized with alarm, and he made haste to the back door, yanking it open to discover what had happened to make her have tears.

Thus was he unprepared for the smell that assaulted his nostrils. The smell of her heat but also the smell of the other wolf, the one who had dared to kiss her in front of him. It was so strong he thought to re-enter the house to grab his sword, but one glance around the yard told Fenris the other wolf was no longer within sight's distance. But then from where did the smell come from? He looked down at his fated mate, and received the answer to his question.

The smell was all over her.

CHAPTER ELEVEN

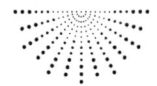

THE sad fact was Chloe was so preoccupied with watching Rafe leave her life forever, and the ultimatum he put down before he left, that it hadn't even occurred to her to worry about their embrace or the smell it left behind. Over the years, Rafe's smell had become so familiar that its presence went without real acknowledgement, like the smell of shea butter in the products she made at home to use in her hair. Or the smell of hay in her chicken coop.

But then Fenris opened the door with a worried look on his face, one that shifted to confusion, and then to such anger, it made Rafe's earlier temper look like an episode of *Mister Rogers' Neighborhood*. Only then did she realize what her hug with Rafe had left behind.

She and the Viking stood there like that, frozen on her back step, each seeming to wait for the other to speak first. The scent of her ongoing heat filling up the air between them.

"You would come to me smelling of him?" the Viking asked her, his voice a cold monotone. "You would give yourself to another while I did sleep then come to me with your need."

"No," she said. "That's not what happened. I was apologizing to him and I gave him a hug. That's all."

"In my lands claimed she-wolves do not embrace men outside of their family."

She pushed past him into the kitchen. "Well, we're not in your village are we? We're in mine. And here, women can hug whoever they want to."

She set the basket of eggs on the counter, and then sprinted to her own room, wishing to God wolf houses were like human houses, where people actually installed locks on the door. Breaking and entering in shifter towns was practically non-existent—who would bother to burgle your house, since any wolf would be able to smell that you'd been there? In the same vein, there was no need to lock the bathroom door behind yourself, because any other wolf would be able to smell you in there. For these reasons, it was rare to find a house with locks on any of its doors in towns like Wolf Springs. The only reason she'd had one installed on the basement door was so she wouldn't accidentally open the wrong door in the night and take a tumble down the basement stairs.

As it was, Chloe barely managed to strip and push her clothes out the nearest window before Fenris came crashing through the door.

Her thought had been to at least get rid of the scent, so she could reason with the Viking. As civilized as wolves had become over the centuries, she still didn't know many who could be reasoned with while the smell of a rival lingered in the air.

And to a certain extent, her plan worked. His eyes, which had been almost murderous in their intent when he came through the door, darkened with another type of desire when he saw her standing there naked.

His eyes raked her body, her newly swollen breasts, the hot wetness gathered at the triangle between her legs, and the next thing she knew, she was on her back, underneath him in her bed as he drove himself into her.

There was nothing pretty about this fourth mating, no compliments, no kissing, no gentleness, only the sound of his animalistic grunts as he moved on top of her.

"I am the Fenris, and thus have I claimed you."

She wanted to tell him again that "claiming" wasn't really done any more, that mates chose each other in her time. But his knot was working its magic against her G-spot again and she could barely think, much less give him a lecture on modern wolf culture.

She hooked her hands over his shoulders and spread her legs even further, trying to hold on and let him deeper inside of her at the same time.

"Yea, offer yourself up to me," he said, driving into her even deeper. "You are mine and will belong to no other."

He took her with such grim determination that when he finally released inside her, it felt as if he had not only mated with her, but also marked her as his.

And knowing this did not keep her from coming. Coming so hard, her teeth clenched together and stars appeared at the edge of her vision as the orgasm washed over her, relentless in its quest to take over her entire body. Despite her earlier shame of being told everyone could hear her, she screamed again. And continued to scream as his hot seed flooded into her womb, her own pussy swelling around his knot and locking him in despite the fact she was pretty sure they hated each other at the moment, that this might be the very definition of a hate-fuck.

The orgasm must have been powerful for him, too, because his entire body went rigid above hers and he called out to a few Old Norse gods she'd never heard of, before collapsing on top of her.

They laid there like that, both breathing hard. The earlier

anger still very present in the room, even as she milked the rest of his seed into her womb.

He eventually flipped her over, so she was lying on top of him. But her new position didn't make her feel any more powerful in this situation, especially when he said, "After our mating frenzy is done, you will direct me to this other wolf's longhouse and I will kill him. Then will we go back to my land."

"No, I won't," she answered.

"You will, or I will knock down every door in your village until I find him and make him pay tribute for his insult with his life."

"I'm sorry, what exactly are you not understanding about the fact that Rafe and I were engaged?" she asked him.

"What do you fail to comprehend about the grave insult of your traitorous actions?"

"Wow," she said. "I have no idea who I must have pissed off to deserve this. Was I Mussolini in a past life or something?"

"I do not understand your meaning. You refer to a person I do not know, mayhap on purpose."

"I mean, I'm a good person. I've always tried to do what's right, and I just don't understand why the universe would punish me this way."

He went still. "You consider our mating punishment?"

"I consider it not what I wanted, not what I planned for. I deserve to be happy, to be with Rafe, and not with some Neanderthal who appeared out of the blue and wants to drag me back to his time where there aren't any other black people or running water."

"I also do not know this Neanderthal you refer to, but I understand it from your tone to be an undesirable thing. Hear me now, I will bear no more insults from your tongue. We are mated, and hence forth you will do as I say."

She let out a growl of frustration. "Oh, my God, it is so unfair that I'm locked with you like this while we're having this conversation."

"Yea, surely you would have me shackled again to your doctor's bed, so you might walk away."

"Okay, try to get this through your thick head. In this time, and in this place, women are allowed to do whatever they want, to be with whoever they want, to hug whoever they want, to be happy however they want. You can't just command me."

His eyes narrowed. "Your intention with these words is to tell me being with me is undesirable to you, that you would rather be with him."

"I'm trying to tell you women have choices now. And no matter what you say or command, I have choices when it comes to this…" She searched for words that weren't "fated" or "mating" and came up blank "…whatever it is."

He gave her an icy look. "It would seem she-wolves of your time do not understand the basic nature of wolf and helpmate, and thus am I right in wishing us to return to my land, where she-wolves are biddable and know better than to embrace male wolves who are not their mates."

"Ugh! It's like talking to misogynistic brick wall." Almost crazed with her own anger now, she physically tried to disengage from him, bracing her hands against his massive chest and pushing her hips away from him with all her might in order to free her body from his. But their physiological lock was greater than her own strength, and all she ended up doing was tiring herself out.

She eventually collapsed on top of him with a defeated plop. "I hate you," she whispered, tears of frustration brimming in her eyes.

His voice was as hard as stone when he answered, "Yet you will do as I bid. I am the Fenris and I will have the last word on all matters between us."

This sounded much more like a promise than a threat to

Chloe. And even though she had absolutely no intention of following him back to his land, to become as slavishly devoted to him as her biological mother had been to her father, she clamped her mouth shut. It was useless arguing with the thick-headed Viking anyway and answering would only restart the argument. Instead she remained quiet, holding herself stiff on top of his chest, until the deep sleep that accompanied each of their matings dragged her down into its dark confines.

That night, she dreamed she was walking down a long dirt road with the full moon shining in the starry sky above. She was happy and nearly skipping in her haste to get wherever she was going, when suddenly she heard a deep growl in front of her and a humongous wolf with a red coat and gray eyes emerged from the shadows.

"Fenris?" she said.

The wolf answered with another growl, this one even more feral than the one that came before. Then he leaped at her, his jaws opened wide—

She came awake from the nightmare with a gasp, and sat up, surprised to find herself on the opposite side of the bed from the Viking. They must have unlocked in the middle of the night and then unconsciously drifted to separate sides of the bed.

The sex they had had the night before still lingered, but the thick scent of her heat no longer hung in the air like a feral entity propelling them along like puppets on a string. Her stomach lurched with the realization that this could only mean one thing.

She, the former fiancée of the alpha prince of Colorado, was pregnant. With a baby fathered by a man more than a thousand years older than her. A man who was determined to drag her back to his time. A man who didn't take no for an answer, and had forbidden her to disobey him in any way, shape, or form.

She carefully removed herself from the bed. He barely stirred, probably more exhausted than she was from not only traveling back in time, but also getting thrust into a mating frenzy less than forty-eight hours after doing so.

For a moment, she was struck by how peaceful he looked in his sleep, lying face-down, his now clean-shaven jaw hidden under his tousled red hair.

She remembered the scene in the bathroom, how he'd looked at her so softly as she finished washing his hair in the bath they were sharing at his insistence, with a shampoo she had made herself out of tea tree oil and castile soap.

"Is there nothing at which you do not excel, beauty?" he had asked her.

And her heart had zinged a little, because Rafe had found all the little things she made and had taught herself to do more odd than endearing. But the Viking had looked at her like he was the luckiest man in the world to have her as his fated mate.

And then less than a few hours later, he had threatened to kill her ex-fiancé and make her do his bidding after they returned to his time.

The memory of that terrible argument and the fact that she was no longer in heat was enough to clear away any goodwill his compliments had engendered within her. And when she gazed upon him again, he looked exactly like what he was. A very dangerous man who would stop at nothing to get his way.

It suddenly became very clear what she had to do now.

Run. As fast as she could and as far away as she could as soon as possible.

CHAPTER TWELVE

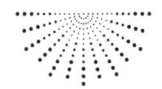

CHLOE didn't even get half a mile out of town before she saw the flashing lights of a police car in her rearview mirror. And less than an hour after sneaking out of her own house with nothing but a laptop and one hastily packed overnight bag, she found herself locked up in the clinic's basement cage.

And less than fifteen minutes after that, the Colorado alpha king showed up.

It took all the manners Myrna had drummed into her not to groan upon the sight of Dale Nightwolf coming down the steps, his long, lean body a twin of his son's, even if his face was longer with more wrinkles.

She stood, which was the respectful thing to do in the presence of your alpha, and mumbled a small, "Hi."

"So let me get this straight," he said, ignoring her greeting. "First you lead my son on for seven years, then you go into heat with another wolf, and then to top it all off, you decide to run away, leaving us to deal with the out-of-time Viking currently residing in the house my son bought for you to live in. Do I have that about right?"

Chloe's cheeks heated. "In all fairness, I did offer to pay Rafe rent. But he wouldn't let me."

He sniffed the air. "And you're pregnant. Well, doesn't that just about beat all?"

"Rafe asked me to leave. He told me not to be here when he got back from Alaska."

"He didn't mean run away and leave your Viking behind. He wanted both of you gone." He gave her a disappointed look. "You know that, Chloe. You shouldn't have tried to run away. You made an already bad situation even worse."

Having her king be angry with her, she could take, understand even. Rafe was his son, after all. But having him look at her with such disappointment in his eyes was almost more than she could bear.

If not for her need to get out of this cage and fast, she would have begged him for his forgiveness as opposed to saying, "You realize that me running away isn't a crime though, right? You don't actually have any grounds to hold me here, under arrest." Chloe had to swallow in a deep breath of bravery to say this next thing: "And just because you're the alpha doesn't mean I have to explain myself to you or that you can treat me however you want. There's no law that says I can't go anywhere I want any time I choose. But the time the Viking is trying to force me to go to doesn't have protections like that. That's why I ran away."

Dale's face went from disappointed to angry again as he took a step closer to the cage. "Forgive me if after watching my son moon over you and let better prospects mate with other wolves for seven years, I don't feel all that sorry for you."

"And forgive me if I don't think your anger is a good enough reason to travel a thousand years back in the past with someone I barely even know."

"He's your mate," he said, shaking his head. "I know you modern she-wolves are all about your rights this and your rights that. But back in my day, a good she-wolf knew how to follow."

She folded her arms and sat down on the bench, not caring how insulting an action like this was to her alpha king. She was so sick of alpha kings from both the past and present trying to tell her what to do. Also, he had lost any right to her deference when he had the sheriff haul her into this cage like a common criminal.

"Well, I guess I'm not a good she-wolf then," she said. "Now either charge me with something or risk me suing you, Dale, and this entire town for wrongful imprisonment in the human courts. You know how the North American Lupine Council hates to see us in the human news. They'd probably make you settle out of court and send the Viking back through the portal yourself."

The way Dale's face twisted with annoyance let Chloe know she was right, and though it was agonizing for her to talk this way to the man she had hoped would one day become her father-in-law, she pressed on. "Release me," she demanded. "Release me now, or I'll make you pay."

He sighed. "You know, I like you, Clo, I always have, from the moment we opened our home to you. But when my boy started talking about proposing to you, I had a bad feeling about it. Not just because you were odd with all that alternative stuff you're into, but also because I looked at you two and I didn't see lovers like Lacey and me, but two four-year-olds who didn't want to stop being friends. I tried to tell Rafe that you weren't a match, and Lacey also had her doubts but she loved you too much to back me up with Rafe. Now look what's happened. You've wasted seven years of our boy's life and you're sitting here demanding that we all bend over backwards to accommodate you."

He all but spat the words at her, and Chloe couldn't mask the hurt they caused her. She had been so looking forward to joining their happy family, and thought Rafe's parents felt the same. But apparently Dale had never wanted her to be with Rafe in the first place. And if what he was saying was true, his wife, Lacey, who she'd loved like a second mother, had also had her doubts from the start.

But she couldn't let her hurt feelings take her off course. She had to get out of this cage and out of town before the Viking woke up.

"I'm sorry," she said to Dale. "I know you don't believe me, but I'm truly sorry for all the hurt I've caused. And I'd give anything for things to have worked out differently. But I can't go back in time to Norway. That's insane. I have got to get out of here and you've got to help me—"

From upstairs came the sound of a door opening and closing and the king gave her a sad smile. "You know, my people still believe in the fated mates spell. We don't question it or try to fight like you're doing right now. So I know you're not going to believe me either, but I am trying to help you."

Just a few moments later, down the stairs came Professor Henley, who had apparently decided to stay on in town after the full moon... and right behind him, dressed in the leather pants she had washed for him, the Wolf Springs T-shirt she had bought him, and a pair of hiking boots he'd gotten from God knew where, was the Viking wolf.

"Oh, crap," she said. It was too late.

※

*I*t took everything within Fenris to keep his face neutral when he came down the stairs and found his mate, as the tutor had heralded she would be, jailed in the cage he had occupied just a few moons ago.

She visibly trembled upon laying eyes on him, but that small salve was erased when she jutted her chin into the air and said something to her king in their tongue.

The king merely looked toward Fenris as if awaiting his words.

And Fenris asked through the tutor-translator that he and his fated mate be left alone. He kept his words simple enough, so the thin wolf would have no need to look within the pages of his bound manuscript to relay his words.

But the king shook his head, and the tutor-translator relayed the Colorado king's concern about the sword in his hand.

"I give you my king's word I will do her no violence, and if you allow this, when you are returned to this place, all will be resolved."

After the tutor-translator gave him this message, the king pondered his request for many moments. Fenris understood his dilemma. The "king's word" was ever-binding, as good as a spoken contract and meant to be accepted without reservation especially by a fellow king. However, Fenris's mate was also this king's subject, and it was a king's sworn duty to protect even the mated she-wolves in his village from any harm.

But in the end, the Colorado king conceded and said through the translator that he would give Fenris a short while with Chloe, with the further warning that they were both in the room up the stairs.

"You may talk to me now," he said to her mind, once the king and tutor were gone.

She clasped her hands at her stomach and stared down at her feet for a rather long and awkward time before answering. "I don't know what to say."

"It appears you would bid me farewell," he said, putting as much softness into his voice as he possibly could, given their circumstances.

Then did she look up at him with what might have been sincere regret in her eyes. For her betrayal or her failure to hie away without his knowing, he could not be sure.

"I know in your time fated mates are supposed to be this big deal, iron-clad thing. And I can't say I don't feel connected to you, especially after what we did, and as... ah... many times as we did it. But culturally we're just too different. I couldn't possibly go back to your time. And you don't seem to want to stay here. And also, you kept on insisting on killing my ex-fiancé, which is pretty psycho, even by werewolf standards. I just can't see me living like that or raising children with someone who wants me to defer to his every whim."

"You would rather have the man you chose before fate mated us," he said.

She shook her head. "You're trying to take this some kind of insult, but that's not what I'm saying. I'm trying to tell you we're just not culturally compatible. In your time, marriages are mostly about male wolves claiming she-wolves or getting fated. In my time, you rarely hear about fated mates. Rarely. Seriously, I had kind of thought it was a myth before you came back for me. And wolves can't just go around claiming any she-wolf they want anymore. We get to choose. And I chose Rafe for a reason."

Again, he kept his face as neutral and his tone as even as he could when he said, "I understand."

She raised her eyes to him, real hope in them for the first time. "You do?"

"I do," he said. "And mayhap there be some manner of things you do not understand about the wolves of our time. Mates are allowed to bid fare thee well. We have only to say these special words: I to thee which I am bound do seek to go back."

"I to thee which I'm bound do seek to go back." She repeated the words, as if tasting them as she spoke.

"But for the purposes of two wolves parting, we must say the words together while holding our hands fast, and in my tongue."

"So all I have to do is say these words with you in Old Norse, and we're over?" she asked, with such hope in her eyes, he found himself in need of a many moments to tamp down his rage.

"If you say these words with me now, I will go back to my time," he eventually answered. He took his medallion from around his neck and once again used it to open her cage. "Will we then join our hands around my sword?" He held up *The King Maker* with his own hands clasped around its grip.

This of all things seemed to give her pause. And he realized why when she hesitantly placed her hands over his own. He, too, felt the immediate tug between them, like a tether, connecting his soul to hers, commanding they be together as fate intended.

"Okay," she said, her voice shaking. "Give me the words."

He gave them to her once, then once again, repeating them slowly, so she might grasp all of the syllables.

"Okay, I've got them," she said in his mind. "Now tell me how to say 'one, two, three' in Old Norse."

He did, and could not help but admire her cleverness when she then said to him in his mind, "Let's do it on Norse three then, so we say it together. Do you want to count down or should I?"

"This I will do," he answered.

"Okay," she said. "But before you do, I just... I just want to thank you for understanding why I can't go back in time with you. And I want you to know I admire how loyal you are to your people. And since this is really the last time we're ever going to see each other, I also want to say even if the circumstances around us coming together were completely messed up, I don't regret these last few days. I've always wanted to be a mother, and you made me feel..." she paused, seeming to root around inside her head for the right words. "You made me feel beautiful."

A part of him felt tempted to say she was beautiful, the most beautiful woman he had ever beheld, and that he had but only put name to it. However, he had already vowed to never again compliment her in the fashion of the besotted wolf he had allowed himself to become over the past three days.

That morntide he had awoken in the manner of a man who had drunk too much honey wine the eve before. At that time, he had regretted his words from the preceding night, and he had resolved to give his fated mate the days she would need to feel more at ease in returning to his land with him.

But that had been before he had stood up from the bed and found her disappeared. Before the tutor had knocked on her door and informed him his "beauty" had been caught by one of their wheeled steeds, attempting to leave her village, and him, behind. And before she confessed she loved another more than he, not seeming to care at all that she was his mate and carried his pup.

No, he vowed, now moving his hands so they covered hers around the sword. He would never again call her "beauty." The only name he would put to her henceforth was "mine."

"At three," he said, as if her last few sentences had not been spoken.

He counted aloud to three and they did speak the words together.

In truth, they may not have needed to hold hands for the incantation to work, but Fenris did not have trust or complete knowledge of the spell's wind, and he did not wish to lose her, the pup, or *The King Maker* to another time and place in the spell's black tunnel.

She didn't see the gate open behind them, and confusion crossed her face when she attempted to pull her hands from the sword. Yet he held her fast. "What—?"

The gate sucked them in and sent them through its black tunnel before spitting them out through his village's own mountain gate, one that had not seen use in all the years of his rule. His aunt rarely gave the fated mates spell, and when she did, it was to she-wolves who had not returned from wherever it took them to meet with their fated mates.

This time when he saw the ground coming up, he tossed the sword aside and drew Chloe tight against him. They rolled into the crash, with him letting his own back take the majority of the hit. And then they rolled over each other four or five times, before coming to a rest outside the door of the gatekeeper's cabin.

Considering the wolf assigned to the cabin was in the position of guarding a gate that saw rare use and therefore did not require true diligence, Fenris was rather proud when a burly wolf showed himself at the door of the cabin with his battle axe raised.

"Lower your weapon," he said, coming to his feet. "'Tis your Fenris."

The gatekeeper, in truth, had only ever seen the Fenris on the occasion when every wolf was invited into the Fenris's great hall to celebrate and be merry. This was always at eve, and truth be told, not very often, as unlike his father, Fenris had seen no reason to spend the kingdom's coffers for such dubious reasons as the return of one of their long boats from sea, or a feast to pay tribute to the god for their harvest, or one to mark the passing of late winter—the Norse wolves could come up with all manner of reasons for these types of festivities.

The gatekeeper squinted now and said, "King Fenris, 'tis truly you?"

"Yea, and I bid thee lower your axe."

The wolf did as he was told, "My Fenris, I did not recognize you without your beard. I bid thee great apology."

"None needed," he answered, "You have well-served your Fenris here today and shall be given reward the next time you come down the mountain."

"How come you to travel through the gate?" he asked. He now turned his squint to the shirt Fenris wore. "And what manner of clothing is this upon your form?"

That question reminded Fenris of the traitorous she-wolf he had left lying on the ground. But before his eyes could find her, a thick boot kicked him in his groin area and he saw stars. The pain was so great it brought him to his knees.

And when his vision cleared, he found his fated mate on her

feet and breathing hard with the exertion it must have taken to kick him in such a fashion.

It would seem she had recovered from their trip through the time gate and put together what had been done. And was she angry with him in the extreme.

CHAPTER THIRTEEN

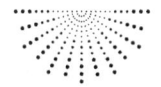

ONE moment Chloe was standing there with Fenris, having just agreed to go their separate ways and the next, she was getting sucked through some kind of pitch-black vacuum, which dumped her back on the snow-covered plateau outside the Wolf Mountain portal. At least she thought it was her portal, until she and Fenris rolled to a stop in front of a small house. Jeb's cabin didn't sit right next to the portal. And furthermore, his cabin was an actual log cabin, made out of pine logs, with insulated windows and a roof also constructed from logs.

The house that sat before them seemed to be made of stones and dirt with a roof made out of what looked like packed in dirt and bright green turf. And then there was the cold. Shivers ran up and down her body. Werewolves tended to live in places like Colorado and Alaska, places with cold weather where their higher body temperatures wouldn't cause them undue discomfort during the summer. But this place—she had never known a cold like this. It couldn't have been more than ten degrees. The harsh mountain wind cut right through her sweater and prairie dress, covering her in what felt like needle pricks and making it hard for her to breathe for a few minutes.

However, all thoughts of her own discomfort flew out of her head, when a stocky, bearded man dressed in loose, rough-hewn trousers and a brown tunic opened the door with some kind of axe raised in the air. It only took Chloe witnessing a few back and forth exchanges between the Viking and this man for her to figure out what had happened, everything that had happened.

Which is how she came to find herself kicking the Viking squarely in his crotch and not regretting it at all when he sank to ground, momentarily undone by the pain she had caused him.

That is, she didn't feel any regret until the short guy started toward her, axe once again raised, hollering in Old Norse.

Chloe's eyes widened and she started to turn tail and run, but Fenris yelled something that stopped the man in his tracks. Fenris said a few more words, and to her surprise, the short man laughed and lowered the axe again before disappearing back inside the windowless stone cabin.

As soon as he was gone, Fenris came staggering to his feet, the look on his face almost murderous with rage. "You will never do that again," he said. "It is considered the gravest of insults for a she-wolf to strike her mate, especially in front of another as you did. 'Tis fortunate I was able to convince him you made a show only because your mind is so addled by the cold."

"I give less than two fucks if I embarrassed you in front of your friend," she answered, coming to stand toe-to-toe with him. "You lied to me!"

"I did as I must after you did try to abscond with my pup in your belly," he yelled back.

"I wasn't trying to abscond with anything. I was trying to get away from you, you time-traveling psycho."

"I know not the meaning of psycho, but understand this word to be insulting in its nature, and as I said, I will bide no more insults from you, Chloe."

"Oh, you think *that* was an insult? *That was nothing.* Check this out," she said before she unleashed a tide of every curse word she had ever learned and few she managed to make up right there on the spot at him. Then she tried to kick him again, but this time, he easily deflected her foot.

"Try that again, and I will—"

"What will you do?" she yelled, holding her arms out at her sides. "Drag me to some time and place, away from everyone and everything I know and love, where I am literally the only black person for hundreds of miles? Because I can't really think of anything worse than what you've already done."

"Calm yourself," he said. "You are fortunate I have chosen to honor our lot as chosen mates after what you attempted."

"Are you not listening to me, like, at all?" she asked. "I didn't ask you to honor our vows. I wanted you to let me go. And you lied to me. What happened to 'we can say fare thee well?'"

"Nay, I did not lie. I spake that *mates* could say fare thee well. I never promised to leave you behind. In addition, it is in the manner of the spell that I could not say it alone and be able to return to my time without you."

"And somehow it all comes down to you, right? Who cares what I want?"

He honestly looked confused now. "I do not comprehend your meaning. What I want should be what you want. You are after all, my mate."

She balled her hands into fists. "My meaning is I'm somebody, too. I have wants and needs and a soul and desires just like you. And maybe I don't want to live in one of the coldest places on Earth, raising pups in a house that doesn't even have running water."

He stepped toward her. "I do understand because I appeared in your village with few clothes and only my sword to recommend me you may think you have mated with a pauper king. But I assure you I have much treasure, and you will have every comfort in my home. Any other she-wolf would thank the gods for their good fortune if they were to be chosen as my lifelong mate."

"Any other woman from *this* time you mean." She pointed to the ground. "Because really, what you need to be doing right now is thanking *my* God I'm a Christian, or I would kill you in your sleep for doing this to me."

"You would threaten me after what you attempted to do this morntide? You would threaten me when you are the one who should be about an apology for your actions?"

"The only thing I'm sorry about is that I didn't floor the gas when our stupid sheriff showed up," she grumbled, folding her arms.

"Again, I do not comprehend your meaning."

"I mean you're used to a certain kind of she-wolf, just lying down and taking whatever you male wolves choose to dole out. But the she-wolves from my time, we don't play that."

He opened his mouth, but she held up a hand before he could tell her he didn't understand her again. "We have a saying in the wolf community: 'Wolves mate for life, so decide how you want your life to go and treat your she-wolf accordingly.' You obviously want to be miserable."

Now he folded arms. "Be aware you are not the only one who has cause to be not pleased with this union. I would not have had the fated mates spell cross my lips if not for being in great need of an escape. It was either the spell or my own slaying at the hands of enemy wolves. And I especially would not have uttered the incantation if I had but known the depth of your talent for treachery."

She held up a hand, "Wait a minute, are you trying to tell me the only reason you came back in time and *ruined my entire life* was not because you were looking for true love or anything, but because it was the nuclear option in some fight?"

"I do not comprehend 'nuclear option,' but if by this you mean—"

He suddenly cut off, his head turning sharply to the side as he sniffed the air.

And though she was angrier than she had ever been about anything in her life, including the time she was left at the side of the road by her own parents, she went quiet, sensing the danger as he did, and even more scary, the scent of five different wolves in the trees surrounding the stone cabin.

He moved to pick up his sword, which was still lying in the snow near the portal. "Stay here," he said.

And that was all he said before he called out something in Old Norse, his eyes glittering with a new kind of anger.

Whatever is was, it smoked out four of the men hiding in the trees. They came charging toward him from all directions, hollering with axes raised high.

Fenris stood his ground, the only indication he was prepared to engage them, a slight baring of his teeth. And then the next thing she knew, he was plunging his sword through the stomach of the first man to reach him, then raising his foot to kick the man, whose belly was now smoking, backwards off his sword. He freed it just in time to duck and catch an axe, which had been hurled at his head, by its wooden handle.

For a moment he had two weapons, until he swung the axe himself, catching his second attacker right between the eyes, before raising his sword with his other arm and swinging it at a third guy. His biceps flexed hard with the effort it must have taken to decapitate the guy with one hand and with one blow.

As the now smoking head rolled through the snow, Chloe couldn't help but be impress with Fenris's obviously superior fighting skills. But then she saw the fourth wolf behind Fenris, drawing back his arm to bring his axe down on Fenris's head.

"Look out behind you!" she yelled into his mind.

But a thrown axe lodged in the back of the would-be killer's head at the same time Fenris turned around, quick as a whip, and plunged his sword into the guy's heart.

Chloe looked in the direction the last axe had flown from to see the gatekeeper grinning over his co-authored kill.

He turned to Chloe and said something in Old Norse, which Fenris mind-translated for her.

"He does apologize for his delay. His mate died many years ago, and he did have some trouble finding her pelt."

And before Chloe could ask why he was looking for his dead wife's pelt, the gatekeeper settled what looked like a red fox with its head still attached around her shoulders.

If not for the insane amount of much-needed warmth it provided, Chloe would have flung the animal skin from her shoulders and made a donation to the World Wild Life Fund just for coming into visual contact with the thing.

As it was, she closed her eyes and let her poor body revel in its warmth before mind-asking Fenris, "How do you say thank you in Old Norse?"

"'Tis current Norse to us," he said inside her mind before saying out loud, "*Pakka fyrir.*"

"*Pakka fyrir,*" she said.

The gatekeeper nodded before turning to Fenris and presenting him with what looked like a cloak made of various animal's fur scraps—but at least there weren't any heads still attached.

"Upon our return to the village you will be given clothing and a fur befitting your station," Fenris said a few minutes later as they walked away from the gatekeeper's house.

"So is that guy going to bury those bodies all by himself?" she asked, struggling to keep up with him, but soon falling behind. He had a much longer stride, and didn't seem all that interested in slowing down so she could walk beside as opposed to behind him.

"Nay, they are in a pile. So he would burn them."

"Were those the guys who were trying to kill you before you used the spell for your quick getaway?"

"Yea."

"You're a pretty good fighter." That was an understatement, but Chloe wasn't in a compliment-giving mood. "I'm not getting why you didn't just take them out like you did at the gatekeeper's place as opposed to coming back in time for a fated mate you didn't even want."

"I had little choice. There were five wolves who would have my head, and unlike now, I was then weakened from an arduous hunt. Even I could not have taken five wolves on by myself. Also, then I did not have the pup inside your belly to protect. For the next Fenris would I be victor this day as I was not three moons ago."

Chloe was finding it hard to believe only three days had passed since Fenris came crashing into her life, like a human tornado, dead set on destroying everything she held dear. "Well, congratulations on the big vanquish. That means you can send me home now, right?"

"My enemies were not vanquished in full this day. Their leader, my cousin. who I also did smell, ran as a rabbit would when he did see his first three followers fall under my sword." He adjusted the animal cloak at his shoulders. "Also, though I am not pleased with you this day, I would not be without a mate or my pup in the winters to follow, so you will stay."

She shook her head. Though the fox fur was now protecting her against the cold, she could feel her heart icing over. "Fine, misery it is then."

If he got that this was a reference back to the quote about keeping his she-wolf happy if he wanted to be happy, he didn't acknowledge it. And they walked the rest of way down the mountain in a silence even colder than the harsh winter air.

CHAPTER FOURTEEN

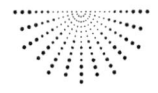

WHEN they descended from the mountain into his small village, his people spilled out of their pit houses, longhouses, and shops to watch them make their way down the village's main thoroughfare to Fenris's own longhouse.

It was much the way he had envisioned it when he had still been well pleased with Chloe. Men and women alike beheld her with great awe, and a few of the children came forward to touch her skin, as if to check if it were covered in paint that might come off. North people were traders by their very nature, and thus, the man who returned from abroad with the most exotic treasure, was the one they talked about when it came time to tell stories around the fire.

He could tell just by seeing the looks on the faces of his villagers that many stories would be told around many fires this night about the new queen.

Many called out to them, and a few even followed behind them, not wishing their story of beholding the Fenris enter the village with his new queen to end just yet. But only his fastest friend and beta wolf, Randulfr, fell into step beside them.

Even though Randulfr was a head shorter than Fenris, his old friend looked more the king than he at the moment, with his red hair freshly combed and dressed as he was in a cloak made of a brown bear they felled two winters ago, as opposed to the gatekeeper's scraps which Fenris now wore on his own back.

"So 'twas true you did avail yourself of the fated mates spell as your aunt did say when we wondered after your disappearance. I will confess I did not believe the sorceress's words to be true and was set to organize a search if you were not returned within two moons."

"You would not have found me, as I had been taken away to a land very far from this one." Fenris had already decided on the trip down the mountain not to talk of his adventures through time, lest his followers would seek the spell for themselves, if only to see, too, the wonders of which he spoke.

"However, treachery was involved in my invoking the spell. While preparing to wash in the lake, I was set upon by Vidar and four followers, three of which I had banished from this place previously. I did use the spell to escape their planned beheading. However, when I did return through the gate, they once again would attack me. This time I felled four of them with my sword and the help of a battle axe well-thrown from the gatekeeper's hand, but my cousin did escape."

"I shall gather a group to scour the mountain now."

"You are well-thanked. Now will I introduce you to my queen."

Chloe received his beta's formal greeting with a distant smile. It was one Fenris would come to know well over the course of the day. She gave it to everyone who greeted her directly, including his family members outside his longhouse.

His aunt was especially happy to meet with his new mate, drawing her into her arms as if they were friends of long past, before directing Fenris to pick her up and carry her over the threshold.

"I must carry you through the doorway so you would not trip

and bring misfortune upon our house," he told her, feeling rather awkward with the vacantly smiling Chloe. "'Tis our custom."

Her answer to this was to lift her arms in the air so he could easily pick her up. But still, she did not speak to him in his mind or with her tongue. And despite his still simmering anger, to suddenly lose her voice in his head felt unnatural and wrong.

But silent she remained, giving but the briefest of glances to the interior of his longhouse, which was not only the largest of its kind in the northern wolf territories, but also well-adorned with bright tapestries along its walls and many bearskins on the floor, so that it was soft nearly every place a wolf might set his foot.

A look of gratitude passed over her face when his mother's sister, Esja, presented her with his own mother's winter dress, a long wool tunic dyed the bright blue favored by her father's people and a silk *hangerok* of red that had most likely hung loose on his mother, but fit about Chloe's curves in a way that made his manhood swell inside his trousers.

However, he could not smell a similar arousal emanating from her own person. Also, her eyes did not light, as a she-wolf's were wont to do, when one of Esja's daughters secured the hangerok's front with two bronze wolf brooches, and then hung between them glass beads and thin chains of gold.

A polite, *"Pakka fyrir"* were the only words from her tongue after her clothing was so adorned.

A pig was slaughtered and set upon his long table for a small feast, to which the local merchants were invited. But there came a point in the night when Olafr, the husband of his mother's sister, noted his queen had not touched her drinking horn of honey wine.

"They wonder why you do not drink," he pushed into her mind. "As do I."

"Women in my time do not drink any liquor when they're pregnant," she answered.

A strange custom indeed, but when he asked her the reason why, she would not give him any further answer.

So he told his family of this strange custom and a drinking horn of goat's milk was set before her by one of the servants, for which she thanked the servant in Norse.

He lingered at the feast, if only to hear her protest that she was tired and wished to return to his bed. But she said nothing more after receiving the milk, merely sitting there with the same distant smile, which never reached her eyes. And the night pressed on with the people around the table filling up with food and honey wine before eventually calling her forth for a song.

"They would have you sing a song or tell a tale. 'Tis the custom of both humans and wolves with new friends."

He thought to this she might not answer, but verily she stood and sang a song rendered in a voice so clear and true, that even though her words could not be comprehended, it was understood by all at the table to be one of heartbreaking sadness.

A somber silence descended over the feast after she took her seat.

"I would have you sing a happier song the next time you are called forth or not sing at all," he said.

Again she did not give him a mind-answer, but reached for the drinking horn of goat's milk in a manner that clearly conveyed there would be no next time.

Finally he gave in and announced that they would retire. This announcement caused every wolf at the table to depart, welcoming Chloe to their village and calling out good tidings as they did so. When they were gone from the house, he showed her to his bed closet and opened its tall doors to reveal the large, free standing oak bed inside. It was covered in furs, and to his mind, seemingly designed to the purpose of holding them within its confines.

"Vikings do not live alone as your people do. We will be given one night of privacy. It is traditionally five, but you are already with pup, so one is all that is required. I would have us lie together now and forget the anger of this morntide."

He moved closer to her, hoping their close proximity might ease the chasm between them at least for this night. He felt warm with all the mead and food he had consumed and she remained the most beautiful wolf he had ever laid eyes on, the mother of his child, and the woman he was fated to spend the rest of his life with.

But as soon as he cupped her breasts over her hangerok with his two hands, she said, "I'll sleep in your bed, but I'm never going to mate with you ever again. So unless you're one of those guys who has no problem forcing himself on a she-wolf, you can remove your hands now."

"We have staunch laws against such things in my land. For the humans it may be practice, but for wolves, I find allowing such causes too much fighting between males who would protect their daughters and claimed mates."

"So we're clear then."

"I will not force myself on you, but if I spoke as you, I would not let my mouth make promises my body might hold not."

She took his hands and physically removed them from her bosom as if dealing with two leeches. "Oh, my body's in full agreement."

And thus, the silence returned. She took off the clothes she had been gifted and slept in the dress she had arrived in, which he had no doubt had been made by her own hand. And the next day she stayed shut in the bed closet, only coming out to relieve herself and to eat the large meal with his family and servants in the main room.

For the first days of her stay, her silence was of such a hostile nature he did wonder if she would do him harm in the night as she had spoken in the forest. But on the morntide of her third day in the village, he encountered his mate for the first time outside of the longhouse since their arrival.

He was deciding a dispute between two wolves over a goat. One had been invited to the other's longhouse to enjoy drink. But in the eventide, the host had promised his guest his best goat if he could do as simple a thing as walk in a straight line to the door. The guest could, though he very nearly fell over a few times before reaching the door. But when the guest attempted to take the goat upon his leave, the host said it was but a jest and sought to take back the goat's lead. Thusly, all three, host, guest, and goat appeared before him now seeking judgment.

He awarded the goat to the guest and then reminded the sullen host that promises made were promises made even if deep in his cups. That was when he caught the scent of his queen and felt her gaze on him.

He looked up and found her still in her Colorado smock with the fox pelt around her shoulder. She had re-braided her hair, and it now lie in one tail down her back. But what he found most interesting was the curiosity in her gaze before she realized he was now watching him watch her.

""You have finally decided to leave our bed?" he said to her mind.

After he said this, she looked away and continued on to the toilet pit that sat behind their house. He might have followed to try to mind talk with her more, but that was when Randulfr arrived at his house with the news that they had not been able to find Vidar in the mountains.

"Mayhap, he has taken to the sea, knowing we are all now aware of his schemes, and that both you and your followers would have vengeance if ever he be spotted in these lands again."

"Mayhap," Fenris agreed, though something in his king's knowing told him this would not be his last dealing with his cousin.

That eventide when he returned to their bed, her mood was much changed, duller somehow. And upon the morntide, she no longer came out of the bed closet to eat, only to empty her bladder, with the rest of her day spent lying underneath their bed furs. When he left their bed the morntide after, she could be found staring up at that wooden carving on the closet's ceiling, and when he returned in the eventide, she could be found to do the same.

It took but two days of this behavior for him to confess her to be the winner of this battle. Verily, he was miserable and he would seek a remedy or it would be a long and cold winter indeed.

CHAPTER FIFTEEN

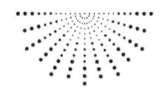

"AUNT, I am in need of a potion," Fenris said without preamble, upon stepping into the small meadow in the forest on the other side of the lake. This was where his aunt received wolves in need of her services in the waning twilight before the night moon fully rose. His aunt he found here, preparing some manner of potion as she was wont to do between visitors.

"Nay," she answered without looking up from the ingredients she was working with a pestle in a mortar bowl.

"But you know not what it be for," he said, frowning at her quick denial.

His aunt let out a great sigh and ceased her work with the pestle to say, "I will not give you a potion that will make your queen forget what brought her here or a potion that alters her temperament or a potion that makes her love you or a potion that makes her obey you in all things. Did you have in your mind another type of potion?"

He folded his arms, annoyed by his aunt's prescience. Even if after twenty and seven winters in her company, it had become more than familiar. "You rather her suffer then?"

"I would rather you fix what is wrong with your mate as opposed to calling on the services of a tired old woman."

"The same tired old woman who commanded me to seek out my fated mate only a few moons ago?"

"Yea, the same tired old woman."

"You do anger me, Aunt."

"Nay, not I. 'Tis your queen who has you in such fine dander. I am but an old woman seeking peace in my end years."

"If you truly want peace, then give me the potion I seek."

She turned to face him then. "Is it known to you how many male wolves do come to me in private, seeking such things? I deny them all as I am denying you. Yet they call me wise woman in your lands and beyond. Why do you think that is, my Fenris?"

"I verily do not know," he grumbled.

"Because the wolves who seek me out do oft listen to me and heed my advice. This is something you have never done, and you are one of the few who do not think me wise."

"It is not that I begrudge you my esteem, Aunt. I simply do seek a remedy to my problem, and it angers me that you refuse to give it."

"I have your remedy. And I will give it, but I would not waste my breath if it is to fall on deaf ears."

"You have my ear, Aunt, and my audience, but considering your fated mates spell did saddle me with a wife who doth refuse to obey, I cannot promise I will heed your advice."

She clucked her tongue. "I suppose this is the best I might expect from you. But you would do well to listen to me in this, Fenris. Your queen is from a faraway place, but her suffering is not uncommon. The wolves who have come to me seeking what you seek have all been the claimers of mates. They say their mates will not mind talk with them or clamp around them for a lay. They do whine because their she-wolves challenge their claims or refuse to show them the respect due a husband after their mating frenzy. These male wolves do beg for a potion that will make their she-wolves more biddable, and I tell them all the same."

She paused with great drama, forcing Fenris to ask, "And this advice be what?"

"If your she-wolf is angered by your claiming, the only thing to do is make her want to be claimed by you."

"I do not comprehend your meaning."

His aunt peered sideways at him with a smirk upon her face. "Yes, I can see you do not. Let me make it plain for you my handsome nephew. You pulled her far away from her lands. She does not know your people or this place, and she does not want to be here. She suffers, which means you suffer. If you want her not to suffer, if you wish her love for you to grow, there are only two remedies. The first is to give her reasons to love this place, to love you."

He shook his head. "I care not of love. In addition, she is the one who did betray me, who did attempt to abscond with my pup. Why would I be the one to grovel at her feet? I am the Fenris, and she should count herself grateful to have me as her fated mate."

"Yea, and if you wish her to count herself grateful, you have need to convince her of your worth." His aunt's tone did hold reason, but something in her smile told him she was also teasing him with her words, which only served to annoy Fenris even further.

"If this first remedy be too difficult for one who does 'care not for love,' here is the second."

She unpinned from the inside of her fur another piece of fabric with different words written upon it and held it out to him. "'Tis a spell to return someone you have brought to your own land back to her own. But be fair warned, once she is disappeared, it will be difficult—nay that be the wrong word—I should say nigh impossible to reunite with her."

His aunt's words burned in his ears as he walked back to the village. How dare she deny him the potion he sought? If not for her advanced age and their family connection, he would banish her from his home for such daring. But then he did reach his own home, which set silent and again this night, empty.

Oftentimes a few of the wolves shifted during the summer months, choosing to spend their sleeping hours outside as opposed to in the confines of the king's house. But as of late, his entire family had chosen to spend the sleeping hours outside of their familial stronghold, even though it was winter. Even his aunt, who cared little for shifting now she was an old wolf, spent these hours outside.

However, the dark beauty's cloud seemed to extend from outside of the closed doors of the bed closet, infecting everyone who entered his house. He, too, had considered shifting at night as opposed to joining her in their bed. Only the certain knowledge of how this would make him look to his village kept him from doing so.

He opened the closet doors and found her once again, where he left her on the morntide, lying in bed and staring at the closet's intricate ceiling.

"You will attract bedsores if you continue in this manner."

No answer.

"Did you at least take meals with my family this day? I would not have our pup starved because of you."

No answer.

Fenris set his jaw before removing his tunic and trousers and crawling into the bed in his linen underclothes.

It was becoming harder for him to believe that only a week ago, they had created the life in her belly on a tide of passion. He remembered the way her wet heat had gripped him, demanding all of his seed, even in her anger. Now they lie there, side-by-side, stiff like strangers or corpses. He smelled no arousal on her, and even her anger seemed to have disappeared, leaving but the shell of the vibrant woman who had told him only her Christian deity kept her from killing him in his sleep.

This is when he knew he must heed his aunt's advice. Even if it was unbecoming of a Fenris. He could not abide any more nights like this one.

CHAPTER SIXTEEN

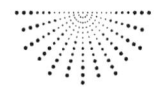

WHAT she missed the most was the anger, Chloe thought to herself. She hadn't realized it had been fueling her ability to deal with being thrust over a thousand years into the past until it slowly ebbed away, leaving only a heavy sadness in its place.

And she had been seriously furious at first, determined to punish the Viking for ripping her from everyone and everything she'd known and loved. But three days into it, she unexpectedly lost her biggest supporter while walking to the toilet pit—which was exactly what it sounded like, by the way, with only a waist-high structure made of sticks to give its user any privacy. As she was coming out the longhouse's only door, she saw Fenris for the first time outside since the day she arrived.

Unlike that day, he was now dressed in a silk tunic top and wool leggings that framed his tree trunk legs even tighter than the pants he'd shown up in Colorado wearing. Around his shoulders he wore a cloak and hood, much like the one his friend, Randulfr, had been wearing when they entered the town, except apparently he had taken out a polar bear to get his coat, because it was white. And just in case there was any danger of someone not getting what animal it was made of, the polar bear's head sat on top of the Viking's own, complete with shiny black eyes and a vicious set of polar bear fangs hanging over his forehead.

Being from a time when polar bears were on the endangered species list and the subject of numerous nature specials, Chloe should have been appalled. But the truth was, with his loose red hair falling in shiny waves around his shoulders and shimmering against the white of the fur, the Viking looked like nothing less than a rock star.

At the moment, he stood with his hands clasped in front of him while two men, standing before him, spoke forcefully, each pointing at a goat tied to a nearby pole.

After they were done, Fenris asked them a couple of questions, which they answered at the same time, each trying to shout over the other until Fenris raised his hand and said a few words. After that, one of the men whooped and went to grab the goat's rope.

To the other man, who had now folded his arms with a sour look on his face, Fenris said a few more words, to which the man nodded before walking away.

She was dead curious about what had just gone down, but realized she had lingered too long at the scene, when Fenris caught her eye.

"You have finally decided to leave our bed?" The thought appeared inside her head,

And that was when the anger started to fade. Because she realized then that while Fenris's people needed him to be their alpha, to lead them, and serve as the judge and jury for small arguments, there was no one offline awaiting her return back in her own time.

Rafe hated her. The entire town of Wolf Springs had pretty much turned against her before she left. Her online fans would miss the *Black Mountain Woman* show, and her sponsors would wonder what happened to her. But Rafe's father wasn't dumb. If too many people started asking questions, they'd just log on to her blog and leave a goodbye note. Her fans would be sad, but no one would truly miss her. No one needed her back in her time like Fenris's people needed him. She had no family, she had no friends, and she had no community, which meant despite everything she had tried to build and do, since getting left on the side of the road by her parents, she was essentially back where she started. A lone wolf in a place she did not know.

And suddenly she became tired, too tired to stand even a moment longer.

She looked away from the Viking and used the ridiculous toilet before trudging back to the bed closet and closing herself in. She fell asleep and dreamed of nothing. And when she awoke, she needed to use the toilet pit again. So she did, and then she came back to bed and stared at the ceiling until sleep overtook her again. And when she woke, it was time for the toilet pit again.

This continued on for how long, she didn't know. On a few trips the rest of the people who lived in the longhouse would be gathered around the table eating, and the same woman who had hugged her like she knew her on that first day, the one with a face full of wrinkles, crisp gray eyes like the Viking's, and a head full of silver hair that fell all the way down her back, would grab her by the arm. She'd press a piece of bread covered with one meat or another into Chloe's hand and wouldn't let her go until she finished eating it and had drunk at least a horn of goat's milk, which always seemed to be within her reach. And that was how she came to learn the Old Norse words for eat and drink, the only two words she knew besides thank you and the spell words that had thrown her back in time.

The woman no longer looked as happy as she had on the day they entered the village. And she regarded Chloe with a mix of sadness and pity when she finally let go of her hand.

Chloe's world became the beige of the bed closet, with her days consisting of sleeping, using the toilet pit, occasionally being forced to eat by a little old lady, and staring at the carving on the bed's closet's ceiling for hours on end. It was a rather intricate scene of two wolves engaged in battle, while above it, a woman with a rounded belly and a man stood facing each other, she with a garland of flowers around her head, he with a crown. The couple was encircled by wolves, all of which seemed to be howling at the moon.

Chloe couldn't help but wonder at its origins. But that would mean asking Fenris, and she still wasn't talking to him, even though he had become the only other spot of color, besides the old lady who made sure she ate, in her days. Occasionally, she'd still be awake when he joined her in bed and the Viking would push a couple of sentences into her mind, usually surly ones, that she was able to take a little pleasure in not answering. But not much.

When he joined her in bed that night, he said, "You will attract bedsores if you continue in this manner."

She didn't answer.

"Did you at least take meals with my family this day? I would not have our pup starved because of you."

She didn't answer, though that did bring her a tiny pin prick of guilt, because she'd need to get her act together if she wanted to deliver a healthy baby, especially in a time period without prenatal care. The guilt actually made her feel a little better. She was beginning to feel grateful for the ability to feel anything at all.

Eventually the Viking came to lie down beside her, his body stiff beside hers, and even though she couldn't see his face, she could feel the anger radiating off of him as she drifted off to sleep again... only to be shaken awake what felt like just a few hours later.

She opened her eyes to see the Viking standing above the bed.

He held out the fox pelt the gatekeeper had given her. "You will come with me now."

She just looked back at him, letting her lack of action serve as her denial of his command.

"Do not force me to throw you over my shoulder," he said, beckoning her with his hand. "Come now."

She got out of bed and took the fox fur from him. Partly because she didn't doubt the asshole would throw her over his shoulder, but mostly out of curiosity. What could he want her to see so badly that he'd wake her in the middle of the night?

When they emerged from the longhouse, a half-moon was still high in the sky, which along with the stars, was all the light they needed to guide their way through the village, toward the small forest that stood just beyond the lake.

They walked together in silence, just like they had when they came down the mountain. This time, however, he slowed his steps so she could walk beside him as opposed to behind him.

They stopped just outside the forest, where a pack of what looked like fifteen to twenty large wolves all lie together in a pile of mostly red, but some yellow, bodies.

He let her observe them for a few moments before saying, "The yellow wolves are our servants and their children, who have all come here from another land. The wolves do take thralls as the humans do as wolves will serve no other, even by force. But if a family has great debt, they may offer themselves at our secret market to serve in the house of another so as to pay it back along with receiving a place to live and food to eat. So have these wolves come to live with us."

He pointed to the red wolves. "These red wolves be my family, my two cousins, their mates, their children, my mother's sister, and her mate and children."

He then pointed to a smaller silver wolf, sleeping near the edge of the pack. "And that is my aunt, my father's sister. She is an accomplished sorceress. In fact, it was she who did give me the fated mates spell. She is also the one who will start teaching you our language on the morrow. You will come out of our bed closet every morn as I do and not return to it until the eve as I do. From this moment on, you are no longer the dark beauty from a foreign land. You are our queen and my family is now your own."

※

Fenris had half-expected the dark beauty to start talking, just so she might balk at his command as she had done when he attempted to lie in the way of man and woman with her. But he received no answer after making his speech, which made him clench his teeth and greatly lean on his patience so as not to demand acknowledgement of his decree.

And when he woke on the morn, her side of the bed lay empty.

He growled in frustration. If she had run away yet again... he didn't finish that thought, fearing the dark place his mind went.

He burst out of the bed closet with an angry yell, only to find the she-wolf and his entire family staring at him from the communal table where they all sat. She was now fully clothed in his mother's over tunic and hangerok, though she had used simple clothes pins as opposed to the bronze wolf brooches she had been given to the keep the straps in place at her chest. He also spied that she was sharing a bowl of porridge and a loaf of bread with his aunt as if the two were old friends.

"My brother's son," his aunt cried out. "You have failed to gift your wife a woman's dagger. She is forced to share my bread, so any passerby would think I am the queen and she the old witch."

Since human women were not allowed to carry weapons of any kind by human Norse laws, she-wolves took great pride in their women's daggers, which they used for eating and cutting. The only reason he had yet to gift his mate with one was because she'd yet to have need of it, spending the majority of her time in their bed closet as she did.

"Nay, have not a worry of that, old woman," his uncle called down the table. "Anyone with eyes can see who be the witch and who be the king's fated mate."

The entire table burst out laughing, including his aunt, and to Fenris's great surprise, Chloe herself. Though she seemed to laugh more with confusion than any real understanding of what had been said.

He took his place at the head of the table, but kept his eyes fast on his mate at the other end. She should be sitting at his side, but he had not become king of the wolves by not cultivating patience within himself.

"I shall see to the dagger, Aunt. In the meanwhile, you will start teaching her our language, so she may better understand your jests."

Her aunt's eyes lit up. "That, my handsome nephew, is a very good notion. Mayhap with time, she might grow to love our land as we do."

Our land and our king, her twinkling eyes said.

But Fenris did not acknowledge the knowing in her veiled words. He still cared not for the notion of love, especially after what had passed in the dark beauty's village. But if getting Chloe to eat at his table and partake of his bread meant he would not be aggrieved to sleep next to her lifeless body this eve, then so be it.

❄

Chloe ignored the smug look on the Viking's face as he dug into the bowl of porridge, which one of the blond servants had set in front of him. He probably thought he'd told her what was what with that command of his and she'd be fully coming around any day now.

Little did he know, it hadn't been his command that got her out of the bed closet and back into over clothes "on the morntide."

No, his threat hadn't moved her at all. Only his last six words had: my family is now your own." Could it be true, she wondered, rubbing her still flat stomach as they walked back to the longhouse. Would his family really accept her as one of their own, even though she looked so different from them and was from another place and time?

When she woke up, she found the members of his household hustling and bustling around the longhouse, the women putting layers on over their smocks, and the men doing the same over what looked like linen long johns. But maybe thinking she was just going to the toilet pit again, they didn't acknowledge her presence. She lifted the bench beside the bed closet and pulled out the long wool tunic and silk apron-like dress they had given her on the first day. After she put them on, she went to sit at the long table, where she'd seen them taking their meals. That got their attention, and they all turned to stare at her.

There was a long moment of confused silence, during which Chloe wondered if she she'd made a terrible mistake. But then his family members cheered as if they'd been waiting for her to join them for breakfast all this time before bursting into excited chatter. One of Fenris's cousins came to sit on one side of her squeezing her around the shoulders in the still-universal sign of welcome. The old lady, who Chloe had now guessed to be Fenris's sorceress aunt, came to sit on the other side of her and started talking excitedly in Old Norse, using gestures to indicate that Chloe should eat from the same bowl as she and indicating the jug of goat's milk in the middle of the table.

Chloe did as she was told, and her depression began to ebb away as she watched the family laugh and talk while they ate breakfast as if it were nothing at all to absorb a foreigner into their fold. That is they laughed and talked until Fenris came crashing out of the bed closet with a roar. Then the room once again went silent until his aunt said something to him. Then an older man, who Chloe thought might be his other aunt's husband said something that must have been a joke, because everyone but

Fenris fell out laughing. The Viking regarded her with cool eyes as he said something to his aunt, who nodded happily. Then he settled into his seat, his eyes all but burning a smug hole through her.

But she wondered how smug he'd feel later on when he discovered while she had accepted his family, she would never, ever accept him. She'd happily learn the language and help her new family out in any way she could. But she'd never give herself to him the way she had back in Colorado and she'd never forgive him for taking her planned life away.

CHAPTER SEVENTEEN

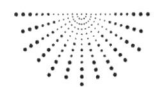

THREE full moons after his fated mate came to his village, she had learned his tongue well enough to speak simple conversations with his family and slightly more complex ones with his aunt, who was patient and would keep her language simple with her student. His entire family had moved back into the longhouse, spending their sleeping hours in human form on the benches that lined his walls as humans and not in the snow as wolves.

And soon did he have a notion his own family liked his queen more than the Fenris himself. He had this notion because they told him as much around the table, full of belly as they were with the flavorful meals she oversaw. After her first day in the cooking area, directing the servants to where the herbs and spices she could distinguish by smell might go, and speaking as best she could what should go in the cooking pot, the servants set forth a stew so pleasurable to their mouths, his family gave his mate great cheer. She was well-thanked by all, and henceforth, they all endeavored to also help her with their tongue because the more herbs and spice and food stuffs his queen was able to identify, the better their own meals became. It would seem her talent for cooking made her as popular with his family as it had in her own land. And she gave glad smiles and words best she could to everyone who thanked her for the privilege of her food. To his surprise, she had come to hold his family dear in a very short time.

But his fated mate had yet to say more than three words to him, and those three words were always the same: No, thank you.

"No, thank you," when he offered her a jeweled women's dagger, more splendid than any he had ever seen.

"No, thank you," she said, when he presented her with a silk dress more befitting a queen. She continued to wash and clean his mother's simple tunic and silk hangerok every wash day herself, wearing them over the dress she had brought with her from Colorado.

"No, thank you," she said when he brought up the matter of her sitting in her rightful place at the dinner table.

Yea, it was better than the ghost of a she-wolf into which she had turned for those three moons before she began her Norse study, but in some ways it had become harder. Harder of both mind and body. Lying in bed next to a corpse had not excited his manhood in the least. Lying in bed next to a vibrant beauty such as his queen, without having leave to touch her was akin to torture. And he again found himself heavy of foot, because though he willed his prick to go flaccid in her presence, it rose like a battering ram at the mere sight of her removing her tunic dress and hangerok in the eve, before settling into their bed. And in this manner he was kept awake by his desire for her, while she slept on, uncaring of the state he was in.

Thus, did he find himself back in the meadow with his aunt soon after the time of the year when the sun grew lazy and chose to stay rested in the sky.

"Your remedy has not met with success," he informed her.

"She has come to love your family and she does talk and eat

again," his aunt answered without question of his subject. "Verily, your pup shall at least be happy with her progress if not yourself."

"Yea, but she refuses to mind-talk with me still, save for when she wishes to say nay to one of my gifts."

"Mayhap you do not come to her bearing the right gifts. Not every woman can be happily claimed with objects that be pleasing to the eye. But they can oft be brought around if the gift be of right sort."

"She is a queen. She can avail herself of the riches in my coffers and will never want for food or clothing. What more would a she-wolf hold dear?"

"Ah, 'tis oft the short thinking of males which have brought about the most tragic endings in the love stories told around our fires."

"I tire of your riddles, aunt," he said, his voice growing hard. "Tell me plainly what I should do to resolve this matter."

"I have already told you this plainly. You should put your mind toward giving her the right gifts," his aunt said. "Once you do, all shall be well between you two."

And thus did his aunt end this conversation, picking up her basket with the claim that she must search for a certain spell plant that could only be found during the time of the resting sun. "If I do not find it before the sun does travel across the sky again, it will be buried under snow, making for a long winter indeed for any wolf who should have need of it."

Somehow he knew this to be a statement about the urgency of his own travails with Chloe. If he did not find a way to mend what was torn between them before their pup came, it would be a very long marriage indeed.

❄

Other than being mated with a pompous asshole, Chloe found herself really liking the Viking Age. Communal living took getting used to, but as someone who had been sadly solo for most of her life, the intimacy of always having people around almost made up for the complete lack of privacy. She also loved that everything here was made from scratch and mostly do-it-yourself. It was like living in an amusement park made up entirely of things that interested her.

The only drawback was Old Norse was super-hard to learn without the benefit of a textbook, dictionary, or a teacher who also spoke the same language as you did. Fenris's aunt was doing a great job of teaching her under the circumstances, but the questions were piling up in Chloe's mind, and even when she could figure out how to ask them, she still didn't always have the vocabulary to understand the answer. This was more than frustrating.

For example, cooking with spices was easy enough, but hadn't been able to incorporate many herbs because she didn't know the names for the ones not made obvious by the way they smelled. And she wanted so badly to learn how to make the unleavened bread they ate with dinner, but there was only so much that could be taught with gestures.

And she didn't even want to talk about all the questions she had about their lifestyle in general. She'd managed to figure out that the longhouse had no windows in order to keep out the cold in the winter and, at this time of the year, the light of the sun, which didn't fully set. She'd also gleaned that the wolves in this place were opposite the ones in Colorado. While they definitely weren't as civilized as Rafe and his crew in their human forms, they could almost be called fully domesticated in their wolf forms. They had full control of themselves when they shifted and they didn't go on animal killing rampages or attack humans after changing. Back in Colorado, pregnant wolves had been giving strict warnings never to risk leaving their house on full moon nights. Here, she could freely walk around the village without fear and in fact, she had done just that the last two moons, missing the presence of her new family at night. During the last full moon she had even fallen asleep in their wolf pile, warmed by the ever-present sun and their sleeping bodies. She would have stayed out there all night if Fenris hadn't come to get her.

But she didn't understand how they trained themselves to be this way in animal form or how they dealt with childbirth. There didn't seem to be any place set up for human medicine in the village, and the few times she had seen a wolf get hurt, they had immediately shifted into wolf form, not coming out until they were fully healed.

She did, however, manage to finally string enough words together to figure out how to ask Aunt Bera about the carving on the bed closet's ceiling.

"Tis the story of the mother and father, from whence Fenris did come," his aunt answered. "They were as you and Fenris are. Fated mates."

She wanted to ask what the fighting wolves meant, but couldn't because she didn't know any words that meant fight. Then she wanted to ask if the carving of his parents with wolves circled round them was from their wedding, but realized she didn't have the word for wedding.

Finally she settled for, "Where are his mother and father now?"

Aunt Bera cackled in that teasing way of hers. "Mayhap, you should ask Fenris."

Chloe let out a frustrated breath. "I cannot ask him."

"You will not ask him. These words, you turn around." His aunt made a gesture with her fingers for turn around, so Chloe could understand her meaning.

Instead of answering this accusation, she used a feather dipped in charcoal from the nearby fire pit to write down the words for "turn around" in her notebook that she'd sewn together from sheets of leftover fabric. The discovery that she knew how to write her own language was met with great awe by the others in the longhouse, and questions about her father's wealth soon followed. Apparently, most women and men were illiterate in this time period with only the wealthy knowing how to read and write. From what she could see, Fenris and his aunt were two of the only people in the village who could fully understand the runic alphabet. Eventually Chloe would learn to read and write runic letters herself, but that was also slow-going at this point.

"My queen, your language would grow faster if you did but mind-talk with your mate," Aunt Bera said now. "That is how foreign wolves who come to our land do learn."

Chloe shook her head. "You do not understand, and I do not have the words to give you knowledge of what is between us."

Aunt Bera covered her hand. "If you mind-talk with him, you could then have the words you need to make me understand. Then mayhap—"

Aunt Bera broke off when Fenris appeared in the doorway of the longhouse, as if summoned by their conversation about him. His eyes soon found her sitting with Aunt Bera, and he came over to them. But he held out his hand to Chloe alone, pushing a thought into her head. "You will come with me, now."

She ignored his hand, but again rose to follow him out of the house as she had the night he had shown her his family's wolf pile. She wondered what he would show her this time. Maybe two bunnies copulating, followed by a command to resume having sex with him again at the evening tide.

That seemed to be his M.O., and she knew he'd been suffering. She had woken up a few times in the middle of the night, somehow enfolded inside his arms, with a rather obvious erection pressed into her backside. And maybe she had lingered there for a moment or two, enjoying the warmth of his arms around her before moving out of them—but only because she hadn't had much affection growing up. At least that was what she told herself. Obviously, she was hard up for hugs and didn't care where she got them or who she got them from.

But if he planned to command her to resume having sex with him again, that's where she drew the line. And even better, she now had enough Norse under her belt to tell him "No, thank you" but good.

However, she didn't have long to ruminate on these thoughts, because this time he actually talked with her while they walked, unlike the other trips they'd taken together.

"This row of longhouses belongs to our traders. They shall return nigh harvest time with the spoils of our trades and stories of lands from afar. Then will we have a large celebration and feast to which all the alpha chieftains in the wolf lands will be invited."

She bit back all of her questions. Like how do wolves manage to travel by boat for so many full moons? Was that why they had trained themselves to be gentle in wolf form? And was it possible to put in a request for spices they didn't have on hand the next time his traders left for market? And what did they trade for anyway?

"After the next full moon, I will dispatch Randulfr and a hunting party to the Northern Ice to hunt the great white bear, so we may have provisions with which to barter and sell when the traders sail again this summer next."

Again, so many questions popped off in her head, but she refused to ask them.

"Ah, here we are at the smith's house."

They walked into a dark room, which Chloe figured out was actually a free-standing, one-room structure, behind which sat the smith's longhouse. The two wolves inside the workshop, one father and one son, judging by the similar look of them, both stood up when they entered. And it seemed they were expecting

Chloe and Fenris to stop by because the older one immediately waved a hand toward a square stone, with a glowing red rectangle on top of it.

She didn't understand.

"My queen, the smith has agreed to show you how he makes the woman's dagger and at the end of your lesson, you will have a simple dagger of your own to use at meal time and for cutting materials and also for defending yourself against wild animals if you should meet them in the forest."

Her eyes widened, and she once again had to squelch her follow-up questions, including whether a dagger could be used to do stuff like shave, and um, what wild animals in the forest? Though, she kind of didn't want to know the answer to that second question.

"I will translate any questions you might have for the smith and his son, but you will have need to talk to me do so."

Before she could even think to say, "No, thank you," her butt was on the stool in front of the anvil and she was asking, "Is there more than one cast for making these? If so, may I choose mine? And I see he's already heated the iron. Is there any way to ask him to back up and start from the beginning without being rude?"

Fenris said a few words and the two men scrambled to start gathering what appeared to be a large set of blackened tongs and a number of oddly shaped hammers.

"What did you say?" she asked him.

"Your queen wishes for you to start from the beginning."

"I said without being rude!"

"He is your subject. In this relationship there is no such thing as rude."

"Yeah, actually there is. You kings and queens just haven't figured that out yet," she answered. "Just be happy you're not French. That lesson is going to get learned like a mofo in France several hundred years from now."

"I did forget how baffling you could be." He smiled and came to stand behind her stool.

She wanted to tell him if he really wanted to understand baffling, he should try learning Old Norse from scratch.

But then the two smiths started pouring molten ore into the cauldron and she became too interested in what they were doing to give him a good comeback.

❄

The next day Fenris showed up after her lessons again. This time he took her to the iron fields to see where "much of our metal" came from. That one was a little less hands on, since unlike women of this age, she knew better than to handle anything with questionable chemical content while pregnant. But it was still thrilling to see how people who had no formal classes, internet, or books to guide them, made things day in and day out.

The day after that, he woke her early in the morning to take her to the farm hamlet just a little ways down the coast to show her where all of their grain came from. The hamlet was relatively nearby, but it was still about an hour away in the small fishing boat he'd procured for the trip, and when Fenris started to tell her stories about the mostly unpopulated lands they passed along the way, she forgot herself and started asking him questions about where the humans lived and how much interaction they had with them. And somehow they ended up talking about the differences between wolf and human interactions in both their times all the way there.

Then on the way back from the hamlet when Fenris asked her if they had the resting sun for a time in her land, that led to a conversation about how she knew a little about a lot of things due to at first to these things called "books" and then later on to a more recent invention called "the internet," which was how so many people all around the world were able to know about what they called "the midnight sun" even if they had never seen it in real life with their own eyes.

He kept asking her questions about "these matters that could be read in books" and "the internet," until eventually she told him the story of how Professor Henley had figured out he was a Viking back in Colorado, and found a picture of his sword at a museum in a city called Oslo, which might have not yet been founded in his time but was the capital or the main city of Norway in her own. And that led to a discussion about what year they were in, and that never fully got figured out, since the Norse wolves used a calendar that was a mix of moons, summers, and winters, and eras of rule, as in "The time of the second Fenris" and the time of the "third Fenris." Fenris was the sixth in his own line of kings, but there was another Fenris line before that, which would take "many boat trips for which to account" according to Fenris.

The day after that, he took her to the beekeeper's longhouse to see how the honey that sweetened their food and provided the base for their mead was made. And so on and so forth until before she knew it, another full moon was just a day away.

To Chloe, it felt much like what she'd seen and read about in human mating rituals. Wolves didn't date and in many cases, they didn't even bother with getting to know each other. A she-wolf went into heat and then proceeded to have crazy wolf sex day and night with whatever guy she either wanted or had agreed to mate with until she got pregnant. Then if they were lucky she went into heat maybe one or two more times within her lifetime, giving her two more pups before they grew old and died together.

Everything romantic that happened between wolves tended to come before their actual heat night. And even then, it wasn't so much dating, as hanging out and deciding if they wanted to be together on their heat night. Not exactly the stuff of romance novels.

Cases like hers and Rafe's, where two wolves got to know each other as adults before the she-wolf went into heat, were rare and Wolf Springs was full of mates for life, who grumbled in their later years that they didn't have anything in common and wished they had chosen more wisely.

But nearly every day, the Viking took her somewhere for at least an hour or two to let her see how something was done or made. And soon the conversations they had on the trips to and from these dates started to spill over into the rest of her life. They'd mind-chat over breakfast about what each of them had planned for the day, then he'd come get her for their "date" after her lesson with Aunt Bera, then he'd go off and do something else on his never-ending list of kingly duties. And she soon began to miss him when he was away to the point where it felt like the midnight sun inside her chest when he came back through the door for dinner, during which they'd mind chat about both their days just like couples had apparently been doing throughout the centuries in both her and his times.

It kind of felt like Stockholm syndrome considering she had vowed to stay mad at him forever just four months ago. But who else did she have to talk to about the differences between her time and his? And the Viking seemed just as in interested in hearing about the engineering feats of her time as she was in learning about the DIY features of his.

"You're a bit of a sci-fi nut, aren't you?" she asked the day before the full moon as they walked along the river which ran east from the lake, through a valley bordered by mountains on each side. Their destination was unknown to her. She liked the surprise of finding out, and maybe he liked surprising her, because he never volunteered the information when he picked her up from her Old Norse lessons—which were going much better now she could take an extra five minutes to ask Fenris the

Old Norse equivalent for all the missing words that came up in that day's session with Aunt Bera.

"I once again do not comprehend your meaning," he said now, but his voice held teasing, not censure, when he said it.

"In my time, there are all these stories set in the future. Like we have a bunch of, um... I guess you'd call them 'tales' set on these things called 'space ships,' which are basically boats that ride through the stars. And a lot of people just love them, love imagining what the future will be like."

"But you do not?"

"I mean I'll go to a summer movie, but I don't read it or seek it out. I'm more of a historical fiction person myself, though it's hard to find historical novels about black people that aren't set in the time of slavery."

They had already had a long conversation on the subject of slaves versus what Fenris called thralls. In both histories, this was fully a human practice, and to her surprise, in both histories this had been one of things that diversified the werewolf population. He'd explained to her all the wolves of Norway sported red hair like he, but when human Vikings started bringing back thralls from far-off lands, that had meant more accidental turnings. In the time before the Vikings took to boat to raid and trade, and before the Norse werewolves taught themselves to remain calm in wolf form in order to be able to do so themselves, the humans who lived in communities nearby knew not to go wandering about on the night of the full moon. But thralls, thinking their new masters superstitious, used this as their one opportunity to escape. Some of them made it out. But many more of them ended up werewolves. That is, if they survived the initial attack.

This was also how black wolves came to reside in the United States, she told him. Africa, or Bland as he referred to it, didn't have wolves, and many of the first black werewolves were runaway slaves attempting to gain their freedom in the north.

"Yes," he said, answering her original question. "Mayhap I

would have great fondness of this 'sci-fi' you do speak. All Viking stories are about the past and told over and over again. Your stories of new things are very welcome to me."

Before she could question herself too closely about the warm feeling that rose up inside of her when he said this, he stopped.

"We have reached our destination."

Laid out before them was a sparkling reservoir of clear water with steam rising up from it.

Chloe clapped her hands together. "I know what this is!" She winced then, realizing this meant their date was pretty much ruined, since she already knew how hot springs worked. "This is awesome, but we actually have hot springs where I'm from, too. There's a resort you didn't get to see right down the road that's situated around a spring kind of like this. Except that one's all sectioned off with rocks and people have to pay to use it. But that's why our town is called Wolf Springs."

To her surprise, he responded to her confession with a grin. "Good, then we will not have to bother this day with lengthy explanations."

And with that he began stripping off his clothes.

CHAPTER EIGHTEEN

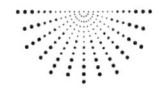

"UM..." Chloe said, quickly averting her eyes when he pulled his blue tunic over his head, revealing the bare chest underneath it, one she hadn't seen in quite a while. "Actually, as much as I would love to take a dip in your hot spring, I can't. In my time it's considered a really bad idea for pregnant women to get in hot springs."

She brought her eyes back to him to see how he was taking the news that she also wasn't going to strip down and jump in the hot spring. But he didn't seem to be taking it at all. In fact, he was toeing off his leather shoes . . .

"So I see you're planning on taking a dip by yourself then. That's cool. You know, I can just see myself back to the village."

"Nay, that is not my plan," he said.

Before Chloe could figure out whether he meant he wasn't going to swim by himself or he wasn't going to let her walk back to the village alone, he was pulling down his pants, and out sprung his considerably large erection.

The follow-up questions trailed away and her throat went dry, right before the smell of her arousal hit the air.

He smiled. "I had begun to wonder if I might ever smell you in this manner again."

"This doesn't mean anything," Chloe insisted, trying to wave away what was right under both of their noses. "I mean, this doesn't change anything."

"You have turned around your words," he answered. "Your meaning should be it changes everything. Now we would both have need of each other."

He took one step toward her, which caused Chloe to take several steps back, only to have her back slam up against a tree she could have sworn wasn't there a minute ago.

The Viking was on her in a second, pressing his large body against hers, so she could feel how hard his cock was as it teased her opening through the skirt of her prairie dress. Before she knew it, his lips were on hers, coaxing her mouth open with his own, and drawing out the kiss with long insistent strokes of his tongue.

It was actually one of the gentler kisses he had ever given her, but Chloe felt like she was under sudden attack. His hands were everywhere, pulling down the frilly top of her prairie dress and palming her breasts when they spilled out. Then one was under her skirt, pushing two fingers into her soaking pussy, which going with the fashion of the day, had no barrier to protect it from his seeking hands.

His two fingers hooked inside of her, just as he pressed his calloused thumb against the bundle of nerves at her center. A white-hot spark of bone-aching need went through her and she arched against the tree, all vows of from-now-on-chastity suddenly forgotten. "Fenris!"

"Yea, declare my name," he answered out loud in Old Norse. Then he pushed into her head: "Do you know how you have taunted me with this smock? It did torture me to lie next to you in bed this winter, and now that the sun is bright overhead, you doth wear it outside our bed closet as well. If you were of a mind to drive me mad with lust, you have met your aim."

Chloe couldn't think to answer. Sparks crackled across her clit every time his fingers moved into her and she could feel an orgasm blooming inside her womb. Then he took one of her breasts, which had become extremely sensitive in her second trimester, in his mouth, clamping his lips around the hard nipple.

And all her barriers came tumbling down as the orgasm rocked through her, making her cling to Fenris helplessly until she melted into a pool of jelly in his arms.

"I had forgotten how pretty you are in your pleasure," he said. "I've a mind to see this look on your face again, but first..."

Again he moved so fast it put her in mind of a blitz. Her skirt was pushed up and her hands placed on the tree for her right before he entered her from behind.

As it turned out, getting taken as a woman in lust was even better than getting fucked as a werewolf in heat. There was no mating knot now, which meant she was able to also feel every inch of his cock, thick and swollen inside of her, filling her up in every possible way as it slid in and out of her slick opening.

"That you would withhold this from me for so long. It is because of you I cannot achieve a warrior's control right now."

And as if to illustrate his point he began hammering into her, his damp skin slapping against her own until he went tense behind her and released. It was all so hot and happened so fast, Chloe felt herself struggling to keep up.

There was now the smell of their combined sex in the air, but still the now-familiar smell of her own arousal broke through that cloud like a tangible thing, insisting on making itself known.

"You have need of me again." He chuckled. "I had a notion the intensity of our three moons in your Colorado was due to the mating frenzy. But I see my queen might have a lustier nature than I had originally thought."

Chloe, who had put years into learning how to be more of a

lady in order to be a good wife to Rafe, wanted to be embarrassed, but the sweet fire of aching need inside her refused to let her maintain her cool, especially when he began rubbing her clit from behind again, as if answering her silent prayer.

"Please, don't stop," she said out loud in English. She begged him. "Just please keep going."

And maybe he understood her, because the next thing she knew, she was on her back and looking up at the blue sky as his words pushed inside of her head. "I will give you what you want. I will give you more than that. As you know, baths aren't as plentiful in our time, because we don't have the 'running water' as you do. But we do have our ways of keeping clean between soap days, especially after a joining. Mayhap this will be our lesson for this day."

His tongue entered her pussy, hot and thick, lapping at her with such precise strokes it really did feel like he was cleaning her up in the dirtiest way possible. And soon another climax began to build inside of her, this one crawling through her, until it felt like every nerve in her body was alive with pleasure. Then he sucked her clit into his mouth as if it was one of the hard nipples on her breasts, and it was as if he'd flipped a switch inside of her. She came hard, screaming out her pleasure in English. The Viking continued to hold her most sensitive area sucked tight inside his mouth until she collapsed back into the ground fully spent.

"Oh, God," she said, when he came to lie on his back beside her. "They probably heard me back in the village."

She couldn't see his face, but could hear the smile in his voice when he answered, "I did have the notion the hot spring might be far enough so the wolves of our village might not be able to hear. But as you know, werewolves have keen ears and you, my queen, are verily quite loud."

She groaned. "I don't mean to be. I don't know what comes over me. I had thought it was because I was in heat back in

Colorado, but I guess I'm just one of those people who's loud in bed. I'm so sorry."

His hand found her face and turned it toward his on the grass so she could now look into his amused gray eyes. "It is you who would embarrass with too much ease, my queen. And it is only because I did know this to be true beforehand that I sought a place so far from the village. No North wolf would be embarrassed to hear his mate announce her pleasure as you do."

Her eyes darkened a bit, thinking of Rafe who she had apologized to for causing him embarrassment often in their seven years together, especially when she was rather clumsily learning which forks to use at the fancy wolf functions she attended as his fiancée. In fact, just a month before the Viking's arrival, she'd spent what felt like an entire night apologizing to Rafe. First, she had apologized for wearing one of her homemade prairie dresses to a dinner party they threw for the visiting king of Alaska and his three daughters. Then she'd apologized for standing in the corner with the Alaska alpha's middle daughter, Alisha, for nearly the entire pre-dinner drinks portion. There were way more Hispanic than black wolves in the United States, and Alisha, her sisters, and her mother, happened to be four of the very few she knew. Also, Alisha, being a history grad student, loved her *Black Mountain Woman* show and blog, so instead of mingling like they had both been supposed to, they spent the entire pre-dinner party cobbling together a version of how wolves might have lived in post-colonial Alaska.

"Sorry, sorry," she said to Rafe when he all but dragged her away from the nerdy history professor.

Then she'd apologized again later that night for defending Alisha's work as a history professor, when her mother started teasing her about not having an intended for her heat night yet. Correcting alpha queens really wasn't done, especially by nobodies like Chloe, whose own status hadn't been cemented yet with a heat night.

Then she'd had to apologize yet again for nearly jumping out of her skin when Rafe surprised her with a spontaneous kiss on the back of her neck.

And then later on when they were alone, she'd apologized for what felt like the millionth time for not going into heat yet.

"Your mind has gone quiet. What are you thinking?" the Viking asked her now.

"Nothing," she answered.

Now his own eyes darkened. "I would know your thoughts."

And she laughed. "Now you want to start really communicating?"

"Again, though I understand your words, I do not fully glean your meaning."

"Communication is a big thing in my time. It's basically couples telling each other everything and being honest about how they feel and what they're thinking."

He scrunched up his forehead, "So neither mate does bid the tongue stay while engaged in this act of *communicating?*" He emphasized "communicating" as if it were a truly foreign word.

"Exactly. But there are rules. You can't be, like, mean or anything. And you can't use it to attack the other person. For example if I'm mad at you for something, I can't say, 'You're an asshole.' I have to say something like, 'It makes me feel sad when you do blank.'"

"And under the terms of this communication, you cannot insult your mate or make him feel he is not the one you want?"

The mood had suddenly become very serious, and Chloe turned fully toward him. "No, you can't. You also can't make your mate feel like her feelings don't matter to you because she's a woman, and not the dominant in your relationship."

"And in this way I would know your thoughts, even when you wished not to give them to me."

"Yes," she said. "In my time if both parties agree to communicate then the silent treatment—that's what we call just flat-out not talking to each other—isn't allowed."

He studied the sky for a few moments before reaching over and taking her hand, which he brought to rest on his chest. "Then yea, I will agree to a contract of communication."

Chloe grinned. To her great surprise, she had found out Vikings were huge fans of contracts. They used them for business transactions, wills, and even weddings.

"You really want to make a contract of communication with me?" she asked.

"If it means I will never have to let another three full moons pass without knowing the inside of you, then yea, yea indeed."

Chloe found herself unable to suppress her giggles. "Well, you know in my time after the birth of the baby, we let at least three full moons pass before we start having sex again."

"In your time, you may not use hot springs or drink mead or handle the bog iron in its liquid form or eat uncooked meat or ride upon horses. And now you do tell me there are also mating restrictions imposed after the birth. I would say your people make the coming of pups more difficult than need be."

She laughed. "You say that but we also have a much lower infant mortality rate than your wolves. For example if a woman went into labor early back in the day, there was a good chance both she and the baby would die, especially if it was breach and she needed something like a C-section. But in my time, Doc Fisher can deliver a healthy baby as early as seven full moons, and if it's breach, he can give the she-wolf this numbing potion called 'anesthetic,' cut it out, then sew her back up. There are also way less miscarriages and even fertility treatments for when a she-wolf goes into heat but can't make a pup."

"I stand corrected then," he said, sounding a little bit sad. "'Tis fortunate to hear you have medicine for all that ails a mother in your time."

"Well, not everything..." she started to say.

But before she could finish, he squeezed her hand. "Let us return to the subject of communication. Now we have made our contract, I would have your thoughts from before."

She smiled, allowing the obvious subject change though she was curious about where his mind had gone before.

"I was just thinking it's nice to be wanted for who I really am. Your family likes the recipes I come up with, your people don't mind telling me all about their trades and how they do it. And you don't find it embarrassing that I scream during sex."

"In truth, I will find it more embarrassing if I am not able to make you do so again," he said.

He then rolled toward her and claimed her lips with his. And by the time they were done beside the hot spring, he was definitely not embarrassed.

CHAPTER NINETEEN

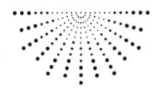

IF Chloe thought the village might pretend that they hadn't heard her screaming like a mad woman at the hot springs—twice—she was sorely mistaken. The Vikings, she discovered, were a bawdy lot, and many of the villagers called out to them as they made their way from the forest to Fenris's longhouse.

"Yea, I can see why you took her so far away. Many wolves might have lost their hearing this day if you had not. You are a true Fenris," called one of the village's lumberjacks.

"I might try the fated mates spell myself if it wins me a she-wolf as beautiful and full of *losti* as your own, Fenris," said one of his warriors.

"Forget the fated mates spell," cried another. "Let us set sail to Blaland now."

Unfortunately, Chloe had learned enough Old Norse by that point to pretty much understand everything they were saying.

"Pay them no heed, my queen," Fenris said beside her. "You shall see the fun of it when another she-wolf has her heat night. In these lands, people do enjoy a good jesting."

She might have taken some solace in his words if his family hadn't turned out to be even worse than the villagers. They kept making strange variations on a joke she didn't understand about Fenris losing his beard. "Surely, we should light the funeral pyre for your newborn beard, our Fenris" and "Do tell your beard to bid our ancestors good-meet when it does join them in Valhalla" and "Has a man ever wanted as much as our Fenris to see his beard not grow?"

They also teased her mercilessly, on and on, until she found herself grumbling out loud in Old Norse to the family she had come to love during their supper, "I would have the full moon rise this day and not on the morrow if it would mean being rid of you."

Of course, this only caused them all to burst out laughing.

"Me thinks you want rid of us, so you might have the longhouse to yourselves," said Uncle Olafr. "You kept Fenris pent up so long, our queen, I have no doubt the only ones who will be getting sleep on the morrow's eve will be we wolves."

"That is only if Fenris finds a way to quell the screaming," said one of the cousins. "If not, we will all be kept awake until the sunrise."

Another yell of laughter.

Unfortunately, her new family didn't have stuff like television, and white collar jobs, and celebrity gossip to distract them, which meant they were back at it at breakfast, and still going when they all came back together for supper before the full moon.

"Try kissing her when she does excite, our Fenris. Mayhap that will keep this night peaceful," said Aunt Bera's daughter.

Then Uncle Olafr set into a rather physical retelling of how he had run for his battle axe, thinking their queen, who he held so dear, was being murdered in the distance—that is until he heard her cry out their king's name. "And yea, then did I realize, nay, she was not being murdered, she was being *stabbed*!" He jerked his hips back and forth to drive home the message.

This got the biggest laugh yet, with everyone, including the servants, cracking up so hard they had tears in their eyes.

She looked down the table to the Viking, who was lazily picking at his plate of chicken.

"Can't you do anything to stop them?" she asked him mentally.

"You have incited them by once again choosing to sit with my aunt as opposed to your king. They believe you are trying to distance yourself from what happened the day before. Embarrassment to Vikings be as blood to bears. It only incites them. Nay, the sole way to stop this is to be bold in action."

She narrowed her eyes, "And how exactly would I do that?"

"A kiss might make for the effect you want."

"So you're saying if I kiss you, and act like I really am full of losti for you, then they'll stop teasing me?"

"Yes."

That reasoning seemed a little backwards to her, but then again just about everything in this time and place was backwards from wolf society in Colorado. She took a deep breath and with her head held high, she strode to the head of the table, where Fenris was sitting.

He in reply scooted back and offered his lap, which she gingerly took a seat upon. Then pretending she was someone else, some saucy she-wolf who didn't get embarrassed at brazen public displays of affection, she hooked her hand behind his head, threading her fingers into his silky red hair before pulling his face down to hers for a passionate kiss that went on and on and on . . .

And Fenris was right. The unexpected kiss completely silenced the room. She could practically feel the wide eyes of family and servants on them as their tongues mingled inside each other's mouths and the scent of her arousal once again rose between them. Only knowing there were children present allowed her to cut it off, tearing her lips from his just as his large arms wrapped around her to draw her closer.

As soon as she stopped kissing him, a great cheer went up

from the dinner table, and the catcalls and bawdy talk redoubled in size.

She glared at him. "I thought you said kissing you would shut them up."

"It will," he answered before slamming a hand on the table, loudly enough to get everyone's attention.

"From henceforth there is to be no more talk of this subject. You have said your part, leave it. And leave us now." His eyes burned into Chloe's. "I wish to start the eventide's activities early."

Every wolf jumped to obey his command, with servants divesting the table of its dishes and exiting the house so quickly, it was hard to believe five minutes ago the house had been filled with bawdy laughter.

"You said me kissing you would stop them," she said.

"And it did," he answered, with a smile on his lips.

"No, you telling them to stop made them stop."

"And I did tell them to stop because you lay your lips upon mine," he answered. "You should try kissing me more oft, my queen, especially the tongue kissing. You might be surprised at what you gain."

Now it was her turn to smile, "So that's what you call French kissing—tongue kissing?"

"Yea, what have the Franks to do with tongue kissing?"

She thought about it. "Actually, I have no idea. It's like the oven, and the microwave, and the bathtub. In my time most of us have no idea how anything works or why we say the things we say."

He smiled, "Then 'tis fortunate you are now in my land, in my time. If you doth wonder how a thing works or why a word is called as it is, you have only but to ask."

She licked her lips. "In that case, what exactly is considered bold here?" She pressed her hand into his crotch and squeezed. "For example, is this considered bold?"

He drew in his breath at the unexpected move. "Yea, very bold."

"Feel free to tell me when I go too far."

"This I will," he answered, his eyes hooding with desire. "And I can assure you now that you have not."

"In that case, if I ask you the Norse word for 'dick,' is that too bold?"

She felt him harden even further under her hand.

"No, it is not," he answered. Then out loud said the word: "*Boli*."

"I see," she said. "And what do you call blow jobs—or is that too bold of a question?"

"I do not know the meaning of 'blowjob.'"

She bit her lip. "In that case, I might have to show you—but I don't want to be too bold."

"I do not believe this to be possible," he said. "Especially considering the depth of my desire for you right now."

"Are you sure?" she asked, even as she slipped to her knees and started tugging down his pants for him. The rush of power she felt from being able to turn the Viking on with just her words and her hand covering his cock, had her own pussy clenching in and out with desire.

He lifted his hips to help her help him out of his pants. "Verily, am I sure. I have enjoyed teaching you the ways of my land over the last weeks. Now I would have you teach me the ways of your land."

"In that case," she said, "There or two ways to play with your *boli* where I come from. The first is I take you in my hand."

She wrapped her hand around his dick and stroked him up and down, just hoping she was doing it right, since her only real lesson in this stuff was from reading erotica and watching a few porn movies in the hopes of jumpstarting her heat.

But she must have definitely been doing something right, because she heard Fenris's breath catch above her, and soon the bulbous head of his cock was shiny with the pre-cum spilling from its narrow slit.

"Too bold?" she asked.

"None too bold," he answered, his voice husky. "See how my cock does water for you. You will unman me in a few more pulls."

"In that case, let's move on to the second form of *boli* play."

When her mouth closed around his cock, taking it as far down into her throat as she could before pulling back to suck hard on the tip, Fenris clenched his teeth and started inhaling sharply through his mouth.

He was so large it was impossible to fit all of him in her mouth, so she decided to try tugging and sucking at the same time.

This time Fenris bucked his hips, throwing his head back and yelling something in up to his Norse gods.

He compulsively grabbed the back of her head holding her there while she fucked him with her lips and hand until he released into her mouth with his third and loudest yell.

She grinned after she finished swallowing. "Tomorrow, you'll be the one who will have to put up with everybody's teasing." Then: "So how do you say blowjob and handjob in Old Norse?"

※

Lying in the bed closet that night, she once again found herself thinking about the carving on the ceiling of the bed closet. Two nights ago she still wasn't technically talking to Fenris and the night before she'd been too embarrassed by the continuous catcalls of his family right outside the closet to engage in any real conversation. But that night they lie blessedly alone and completely sated by what had happened in the chair and then on the table and then again on the benches, and then finally one last glorious time in the bed closet, with Fenris grinding into her slow and hard, until he pulled an orgasm out of her that made it feel like her world was coming apart, that she was shattering and reforming with every stroke.

"What does this carving on the bed closet ceiling mean?" she asked him as they lay there, listening to the howls of wolves outside the longhouse doors.

She felt him stiffen beside her. "'Tis my mother and father," he answered.

"On their wedding day?" she asked.

"Yea, wolves did come from far and wide to celebrate the marriage, for it united two long time warring clans. The father of my father did manage to unite most of the wolves of the Northern wolves under one king. But in my father's time of rule, there did be one chieftain to the north of us who would not bend. He insisted on keeping his pack separate and said he would never pay tribute to any king. It was a stalemate, yea, that could only end with the blood of the king or the chieftain.

"My father would be an honorable man and did refuse to attack such a small village with his warrior force. He offered to the old alpha that they would fight, wolf to wolf, as it did go in the days of old before the time of long boats and Viking warriors. This to us is still the most honorable way. And the chieftain he did accept, much to the upset of his eldest daughter, who loved her father as a daughter is wont to do and did not wish to lose him even though he did stand a wolf of many years.

"The eve of the fight, my father lay in a nearby meadow with his men, and they all fell asleep as the quarter moon did rise. But when they woke up, my father, the king was disappeared. Immediately did they suspect foul play from my mother's village and raise up in arms to either find or avenge their king.

"But when they did come roaring into the village, they found its people gathered outside the old chieftain's longhouse, including the chieftain himself. From inside could be heard the sound of two wolves laying together. It did be my father and the daughter of the old chieftain. She had gone into heat the night before and my father could smell her to be his fated mate all the way from his camp. He did walk from his warriors, past the sleeping guard with none the wiser. So what was to have been a final and grievous battle became a mating that went on for five moons before the lovers did emerge. And thus did my mother become a peace pledge. After their mating, it was contracted that the chieftain's village would remain free in exchange for the hand of his daughter. To this day my mother's village calls no wolf king, and once a season I travel there to hear cases from wolves from all around the Northern lands. It is considered a land of peace, where judgment may be given without battle."

"They're neutral. Kind of like Switzerland," she said.

"I do not know the region of which you speak."

"Um, you know what, never mind. It would take way too long to explain," she said, laughing.

But when her laughter died down, she felt compelled to ask. "What happened to your parents? Why aren't they here with you?"

"My mother did die a few full moons after the day depicted here," he said. He took her hand and laid it on his chest before covering it with his own. "Twas her misfortune that the childbirth of our time 'tis not the childbirth of your time. I survived my birth, but she did not."

Guilt erupted inside of her, thinking about how much pain it must have caused him to have her tell him how much better pregnancy was in her time than his. "I'm sorry about your mom."

"As was my father. He did become a king in name only after the loss of his fated mate. He partook of too much mead and would solve all disputes with items from our coffers rather than battle. I was left to my Aunt Bera to raise, and any greatness I learned of him did come through stories of his past. The only contact he had with me was to watch me practice at sword. I will confess this did make me work at my sword art that much harder, and did I spend much of my time dreaming up new sword tricks to impress my father. But then one morning tide, when I was but fourteen winters, he did come with one of his largest warriors to the place where I practiced the sword with the old warrior he had set to tutor me in weapons.

"My father did push the man into the circle. Then did he put a call to the village to come see us fight. At first I thought this meant to be a display of my skills. And I confess I beamed with the pride of a boy to have my father expect so much of me. But then my father spake the words, 'to the death.' And before I could comprehend, he spake the words of battle start, and the warrior, who did not want to lose his life to a young boy, did come at me."

She clapped her free hand over her mouth, horrified by this turn in the story. "Then what happened?"

"Then did I kill this warrior ten winters older than me and, because I had yet to come into my manhood, almost twice my size. While the village cheered me, my father left to our longhouse without a word. And on the morning tide, we did discover his bed closet empty. After the winter did thaw, his body was found on the mountain."

He took a moment here, obviously finding this part of the story particularly hard to recount. "You don't have to finish," she told him.

"Yea, I do, 'tis the terms of our communication contract." He squeezed the hand he was holding to his chest. "It would take another twelve full moons for me to come into my manhood. But it only took six full moons for word to spread about the disappearance of my father and for every manner of alpha chieftain to come challenge me for the kingship of the wolves."

Now his voice turned sinister in the dark of the closet. "I did fight them all, and when I did come into my manhood, so did I gather an army, travel to the villages of the alphas who had challenged me, and raze them, letting that be a lesson to any other wolf who would think to do the same."

"Wow," she said. "No wonder you're not a fan of fated mates."

"Nay, I do not wish to lose myself in you as my father lost himself in my mother."

Chloe thought about the doleful look on her mother's face as she took her out of the car at Wolf Springs just an hour before the full moon rose. "It's going be cold for a little while, but then you'll shift and after that, you turn back and go up to that shifter town. That's where the king lives, so he's got to take you in," she'd told Chloe. Then in a moment of conscience, she squatted down and put her hands on Chloe's shoulders. "I'm sorry for this. But your daddy don't want you and I love him too much to be without him. You'll understand how it is to love your mate too much when you're older and have one of your own."

But even back then, as young as she was, Chloe knew she wouldn't understand, would never understand how a mother could love a father so much she would abandon her child.

"No," she said to her Viking at that moment. "I don't want to lose myself in my fated mate either."

"Then we are agreed," he said. As if reading her thoughts, he moved their hands to lay on top of her now slightly-rounded belly and the life growing within. "We will be mates, but we will leave the insanities of eros to other wolves."

"Agreed," she said, meaning it with every inch of good sense she had. So then why did it feel like she had just told a bold-faced lie?

❋

The next day when Fenris once again came to collect her after her Old Norse lesson, Chloe was somewhat surprised. He hadn't come the day before, and she'd assumed there wouldn't be any more dates now he'd achieved his objective of getting back his sex privileges. It had been a little disappointing but not surprising, given wolves weren't naturally inclined toward wooing in the first place.

So when he showed up at her lesson that day, she not only got caught up in the pleasant surprise of seeing him here, but she also forgot herself and pulled him down for a kiss after saying hi.

He returned it lustily, pushing into her mind, "Mind the boldness of your tongue, beauty, or I shall take you to the bed closet as opposed to our appointment."

A great cheer went up from the longhouse's occupants, including his aunt, who patted her on the back and said something in Old Norse, which could be loosely translated as "Get it, girl!"

"I thought you commanded them not to catcall me anymore," she said.

"The wolves in my family can only be commanded so far," he answered, his voice as dry as a desert.

They exited the longhouse to much heckling, but as they did so, she could hear one of Fenris's male cousins ask his aunt if he might have the words to the fated mates spell himself.

❄

*S*ince first their eyes did meet, Fenris had heard his fated mate squeak when she shot him with her tranquilizer gun, and screech when he tricked her into coming to his lands, and scream when they lay together. But never had he heard her squeal. Not until he escorted her into the weaver's shop.

"Yes! Yes! Yes!" she said, jumping up and down. "I was hoping for the loom, but I didn't want to ask you for it."

"You mean you did stubbornly refuse to ask."

"Potato, po-tah-to."

"I do not comprehend the meaning of your words, but I would point out that you might have gotten what you wished for all the sooner if you had only but asked."

"Whatever." She let out another long squeal. "I'm too happy to argue with you about this." She then sang out loud in her own tongue: "We're going to make fabric! We're going to make faaaa-bric!"

The weaver laughed. "I do like your foreign queen, my Fenris."

"As do I," he answered in Norse, trying to keep the smile off his own face and failing badly. To his mate who was now doing a dance that included pumping her fists back and forth in front of her chest and pressing her feet backwards in some manner of skipping step, he said. "Now may you sit. There is much fabric to be weaved these next few moons. A messenger did arrive by horse this morn to tell us our ships are due to return in less than three full moons. Remember I did say there would be a celebration then."

She clasped her hands together and said out loud in tentative Norse: "We will be weaving fabric for my dress to wear to a celebration?"

Fenris and the weaver exchanged a look. "In a manner, yes."

"Oh, can we make enough so the rest of the women can get new dresses, too?" she mind-asked him. "I'll feel weird if I'm the only one wearing a new dress at this big party."

"You shall not, beauty, I assure you," he answered.

She crooked her head at him with an exasperated look on her face. "With all due respect, you might have been born in this time period, but you don't know women like I know women. It's not cool if only one person in the house gets to dress up for the big party."

"I know not the meaning of 'cool,' but I assure you the other women in our household will not begrudge you this fabric."

"Why? Because I'm the queen?"

He took rather smug pride in answering, "No, the reason be because this fabric you will be making over the next few moons will be for your wedding dress."

CHAPTER TWENTY

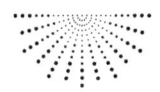

FENRIS did not realize how bad his mood had become until he nigh killed his fastest friend. Randulfr was recently returned with many white pelts from the most northern lands, and had requested to join him in his morning weapons exercises, wishing to engage a wolf after fighting the white bear for so many full moons.

Usually Fenris welcomed the challenge of sparring with a warrior near to his own skill level, but on this morn, every swing from Randulfr's sword felt like an insult. And soon the fighting became more serious than intended with great clanging of their swords and much sweat on both their parts.

Finally, Randulfr backed away and said, "I would have an end to this play."

"Nay," Fenris said, "I would have you continue to fight."

"I am not in prime spirits, having stepped off the boat only yesterday."

"Lift your sword."

Fenris advanced on him, attacking in the expectation Randulfr would defend himself as opposed to wasting his breath with further protest. But then he ended up using all his strength to stop the blade just short of his friend's neck when Randulfr dropped his sword to the ground in the known sign of surrender.

Fenris lowered his own sword, having to resist the urge to punch his friend in the face for refusing to fight any further. "You disappoint me."

"Nay," Randulfr answered, with a knowing grin. "Your prick does make you fast to anger. Do I need to be the one to suggest you find your queen and set her to screaming?"

"She is otherwise engaged these moons. Big with our pup and making many preparations for our wedding."

Randulfr picked up his sword and re-sheathed it at his waist. "Then if I were my Fenris, I would bid her pause. You are in need of a lay."

"I am in need of a fight," he all but growled back.

But Randulfr was already walking away, "Nay, a lay," he called out almost like a song, without bothering to look back.

❅

When Chloe first traveled back in time, it hadn't occurred to her she'd have two skinny blonds washing her hair every Saturday, but apparently the servant women washing all the other women's hair was a thing on Saturdays. She'd actually concocted a sort of conditioner out of eggs, honey, almond oil (thank goodness she had learned how to make it for a Black Mountain Woman show), and a yogurt-like food called skyr. And as it turned out, teaching them to finger comb it through her hair every wash day hadn't been too hard.

The only problem was she was now having a hard time making a big enough batch of it every Saturday. Fenris's young girl cousins had tried her conditioner a few months ago and had been shocked at how shiny and lustrous their locks turned out after air-drying. And soon all the other women in their household wanted to try it. Then because the males, contrary to the way Vikings were often depicted in the movies, were even vainer about their hair than the ladies, they'd demanded a weekly batch for themselves. Somehow word spread and folks started showing up at the door, offering all sorts of trades for conditioner. Which was how Chloe found herself spending most of her Saturday mornings overseeing the preparation of pots of conditioner and preparing for a wedding at the same time.

"It would seem you would have a trade in any time you did set foot," Fenris teased her two Saturdays ago when she clumsily climbed over his body to get out of bed at the crack of dawn.

It was true. Over the last few weeks, Chloe had worked harder than she ever had in her life. Though she was a queen, nothing came easy in the Viking village. She had to make the fabric for her wedding dress, then sew it all by hand. She also had to plan the menu for the big wedding feast, which meant overseeing the roasting and spicing of boars, ducks, goats, and apparently a couple of sharks—which she hadn't been able to convince her family not to serve, though at least she'd been able to draw the line at horse meat. She also had to pre-memorize her vows in Old Norse and learn to do a few traditional dances expected of the bride and groom. The last few weeks, she'd been rising at the crack of dawn every morning and falling into bed exhausted to her very bones every night.

And she loved it.

Unlike the wedding she would have been harangued into having with Rafe, which would have been catered by the most sought after chef in Colorado, and overseen by the most exclusive wedding planner Rafe's mother could find, with a wedding dress provided by a designer everyone recognized by name; her wedding was everything she'd always dreamed it would be. And in many ways it felt like she had been planning her whole life for this.

The only thing she did mind, was she'd barely had a chance to do so much as mind-chat over dinner with Fenris, and even though they slept in the same bed closet, she found herself missing him.

"Is it your plan to wash Fenris's hair at the hot springs then?" Aunt Bera asked when Chloe rushed out of the lake as soon as the servants were done rinsing the conditioner out of her loosened curls and started putting her wet hair back in its side braid while sitting on the bank. Whatever modesty she might have had about sitting around naked in front of a bunch of other women in Colorado had been killed after six months in no-privacy Viking Norway.

"No, after I braid my hair, I will return to the house to sew my wedding dress some more."

"Let us put thread to your wedding dress this day," his mother's aunt said. "We would not have Fenris grow his beard again."

She scrunched up her face. "I do not understand your words."

One of her girl cousins came to stand by her mother. "Before you came to this place, we did call our king Fenris the Serious. Never smiling he, never one to let us feast in celebration, not even for a harvest."

"Why think you I was so keen for him to avail himself of the fated mates spell?" Aunt Bera asked.

The cousin continued, "But now you have cut off his beard again, he is allowing feast, and we hope to have his ear for another at the winter to mark the yule-tide, and mayhap another one at the beginning of the resting sun."

"Wait," she said in English. Then she remembered herself and switched back to Old Norse. "What does his beard have to do with it?"

"When first he did return, we did tease him mightily about being without his beard. And on that first eve he said in your land the men do not care for beards and so do not the women, and that was why it was removed," the cousin said.

Her mother chimed in then. "We all would be surprised, because no Northman would be without his beard in these lands, human or wolf. We realized our Fenris must hold you dear indeed, if he would allow you his beard. But then his beard did grow back and did he become both serious and quick to temper until you did start screaming every few moons. And at the next wash day his beard was once again disappeared."

"But now it does grows back for a sennight or more," Aunt Bera said, her tone growing dire. "We would not have his beard back. We would wish it good-ghost if it doth mean a less serious king."

Chloe laughed and was about to deny any part in the state of Fenris's mood, when he pushed into her mind. "We shall be met at the longhouse. I would have my grooming attended to."

Chloe's eyes narrowed at the women in the lake. Was there some kind of family version of wolf telepathy she didn't know about? "Um … hi," she mind-spoke back to Fenris. "Do you mind washing your own hair today? I'm at the lake and I still have to—"

"We shall be met at the house."

So Chloe pulled on her prairie dress and walked back to the house, where she found him standing in the door in only his pants and his sword strapped across his back.

"Where be your woman's dagger?" he asked as she walked up the longhouse. "We have spoken of this. What if you be met with some manner of animal while you pick herbs in the forest?"

"Then it would probably kill me," she answered. "You saw what happened when you tried to take me on that field trip to the sheep farm and they slaughtered that poor little lamb. Me and up-close-and-personal animal killing don't exactly go together."

He gave her what she'd probably call a "much aggrieved" look, if she were speaking in Old Norse, and then walked past her, leaving it to her to follow.

"Are you angry with me?" she asked a little while later as they approached the hot springs in gloomy silence.

"Nay," he answered between gritted teeth.

"Because if this is about me not washing your hair these last couple of weeks, you should know I'm super-busy with all the stuff that needs to get done for the wedding."

"I do repeat, I am not angry with you."

"Well, you snapped at me about the dagger, and you didn't even laugh at my self-deprecating sheep farm comment—which was pretty funny."

"Chloe, I hold no anger toward you."

She twisted the side of her mouth, "But see, I think you do—"

She wasn't able to finish, because he suddenly turned her around, placing her hands on the rowan tree beside the hot spring before whipping the skirt of her dress up. And then he was inside her, his fingers clawing into her hips, as he pumped into her.

As she'd grown big with the baby, they'd developed different positions for different places, against the tree while at the hot spring, on hands and knees on the benches and floors, and reverse cowgirl—a position that had particularly blown Fenris's Viking mind—for the bed closet. Usually Fenris took his time with her these days, careful with her and with the baby.

However, that day he slammed into her mercilessly, as if crazed and out of control. And her she-wolf loved it. Howled inside of her for more, even as he drove into her hard and rough. "Yes! Yes!" she said in English. "That feels so good, Fenris. More, more!"

It was all she could do to hold on to the tree as the orgasm washed over her, fierce and breathing like a beast coming alive within her. "Fenris," she cried out. "Oh, Fenris."

He let out an angry roar, and she felt him spilling hot ropes of cum inside of her, his cock pulsing between her folds as his large rough hands held tight to her hips.

But to her surprise, as soon as he had fully released, he pulled out of her, letting go of her hips with a disgusted growl.

"Did I hurt you?" he asked.

"No." She turned around just in time to see him kick off his shoes and pants, which were pooled around his ankles.

"And the pup? He is unharmed?" He unbuckled his sword and also let that fall to the ground.

"He's kicking up a storm like, 'Hey, what just happened?' But other than that, he's fine. Are you okay?"

His face was now a grim mask. "I am sorry I took you in this manner."

"My she-wolf isn't." She cupped a hand around her mouth and whispered, "Don't tell her I told you, but I think she might like the rough stuff."

His answer to that wasn't to laugh but instead to turn and do a running dive into the hot spring water, leaving her there to awkwardly adjust her skirt.

By the time she made it over to the bank, he was lathering soap under his arms and over his shoulders. He looked angry, truly angry. And she had no idea why. "Did I do something wrong?" she asked him.

※

When his queen came to stand above him at the hot spring's bank, he lathered the soap over his chest, refusing to meet her eyes. "You did speak truth. You will probably be safe to return to the village without your woman's dagger. You may take your leave now. I will attend to my own grooming."

But she remained where she was. "Did I do something wrong?" she asked again.

He gave the air an exasperated glance. "No, you have done nothing wrong. Return to the village, so you may finish your wedding preparations."

Her answer to that command was to carefully lower herself down to the ground and crisscross her legs under her swollen belly, "I thought we were getting along now."

He gritted his teeth. "We are." He turned away from her, soaping himself in the opposite direction, hoping that would put an end to the conversation.

But she said behind him, "Then under our communication contract, I *would have your thoughts*."

He slowly turned around to face her unable to keep his annoyance off his face.

"Be there need to know my thoughts when there is so much for you to attend?" he asked.

"Just the fact that you're acting like you care how much I have to do is setting off my alarms, Fenris, so come on, spill."

"I know not this 'setting off alarms'—" he began.

"You're stalling."

Indeed he was. But how to tell her in words his feelings when he did not understand them himself? "I did try," he confessed.

"You tried what?" she asked, shaking her head.

"You think I saw not all the work you have been doing, that I care not for your well-being or what you would want. But I did see you have been tired of body and slowed in your actions because of our pup. I am a wolf but I did not want to act the animal. And I did try to stay away from you, to give you the days you did need to make ready for our wedding. It nearly drove me mad."

She folded her hands on top of her belly. "So let me get this straight. You're angry now because you were so horny?"

"I know not the meaning of 'horny.'"

"Full of *losti*."

He shook his head. "Tis not *losti*, that is what does irk me. A Viking warrior can ignore *losti*. I have felt it before and did shove it aside when it meant getting a thing done. No, my upset comes from—" he broke off. "I have no wish for the poison of the fated mates, but I find myself unable to fully resist it. I cannot resist you. You are inside of me, and even when we are apart, with you is where I long to be."

She looked down at him, and for many moments nothing was said accept by the birds in the trees. But then she whispered in his own tongue, *"Hvart elskar pu mik?"* Do you love me?

He had not thought of it that way. Love in his mind, 'twas but a word featured in the songs of the traveling skald, and then mayhap, only because it made human women swoon and offer their wares to its singer after the great feast, at which he performed.

He did not care for this love, did not want to believe in its existence, but as soon as she asked him this question in his own tongue, he knew the answer to be yes. And under the communication contract, he said, "Yea, I am in love with you, but I fear you are still in love with another."

Another long silence passed, in which his fated mate sat, looking as if he had slapped her.

He hefted himself from the water and sat on the bank beside her just close enough for him to feel the heat from her body, but not close enough for their skin to meet.

"I am aggrieved this has happened, too," he told her. "But now that I have put a mind to it, I believe I have been in love with you for a great number of moons. When we did first come to this place and you would not mind-speak or leave our bed closet, my aunt did give me words I might use to break the fated mates spell and send you back to your own time on a scrap of fabric. Yet, did I not use them. They remain pinned to my winter fur."

She turned to him, with tears brimming in her eyes. "So even when I was crazy-depressed and not talking to you, you never considered using it?"

"No, and that is how I have come to realize now how much I truly love you."

He braced himself for her anger, but it never came. Instead she did the one thing that could hurt him the most. She started crying.

Quiet tears fell down her face, and she rocked back and forth with her hands around her stomach.

"I am sorry you still love the other wolf," he said, his heart growing stony with regret for confessing his feelings. "But I still cannot let him have you."

"No, I don't love Rafe," she said through her tears. "I mean I love him but not in the way of mates. I love him like you love Randulfr. As a dear friend. Only imagine if you and Randulfr weren't both friends and the girl version of him asked you to mate before her heat night."

"That would be impossible," he answered. "Girl and boy wolves from different houses have no reason to become as fast of friends as myself and Randulfr."

She dismissed these words with a wave of her hand. "Yeah, yeah, yeah. But in my time period, girl and boy wolves go to school together. In fact, we don't do anything but receive tutoring in the same place for nine full moons straight, six hours a day or more, from the time we're six winters to the time we're eighteen. So please try to expand your mind just enough to understand Rafe and I could have become as fast of friends as you and Randulfr. And if you were in my position, it would have been easy to mistake that friendship for love, especially if you lived in a time when fated mating was fairly uncommon."

She laid her hand on his arm now. "The day I hugged Rafe—it wasn't because I still wanted him over you, it was because I felt like I had betrayed him. It was because I didn't understand then what true love is. But now I do."

Now it was she who reached for his hand and laid it over her heart, covering it with her own. "Because of you. You've given me a family and the way of life I yearned for, and now you've given me your love. I love you, too, Fenris, more than I ever thought possible and to the end of time and back."

His heart swelled to hear these words fall from her lips, but he still did not understand: "Then why do tears continue to fall from your eyes?"

She squeezed his hand against her chest. "When I was a pup of four summers, I was living in a small wolf settlement, somewhere in Washington, I think. My mom went into heat when she was only fifteen, and she and my dad didn't have much money. Plus, they were overwhelmed with having to take care of me."

"Did they not have family to help them with your raising?" he asked.

"Wolf families from my time aren't like wolf families from your time. We don't all live together like you do. And if a she-wolf chooses to mate with a wolf her parents don't approve off, they disown her—kind of like how you banish wolves from the village for crimes."

He shook his head. "That is not like our way at all. As king I only banish if the crime is grievous. If it be but a mating unapproved, the family must accept it and continue on as a family."

"Yeah, that's really not how it works in my time. In my time, if you go into heat like my mother did and go running straight to the wolf who sells drugs to humans as his main hustle, then they pretty much kick you out. But my mom found out quick how uncool living with a drug dealer could be. " She shook her head. "My first memories are of trying to stay quiet and make myself very small, so they wouldn't get mad at me, but it didn't help. They were always angry, yelling at each other, yelling at me, or behind closed doors, doing something I would only later come to understand was fucking.

"But one day it all came to a head. They got to yelling at each other so loud I went and hid in my room and covered my ears, but it was still loud enough for me to hear my dad tell my mom that either she got rid of the kid or he was going to leave her."

"Yea, I see," he said, nodding. "Your parents parted ways because your father did not wish to do his duty. In our village, when this happens, we send the young wolf on an ocean voyage, which is oft enough to make him see the lure of hearth and home. But I would guess you do not have such a practice in your time and it must have caused you great sadness when your parents parted."

She looked up him. "They didn't part."

He shook his head, confused. "Then why does this memory continue to sadden you to tears?"

"Oh, my gosh, you can't even fathom, that's so…" And to his surprise, she began to have tears again. "My mother chose him. She left me by the side of the road and drove away with him. That's how I came to be in Wolf Springs, that's why I don't have a family of my own, and that's why it moves me to tears when you say you're never going to let me go. I didn't know until now how much I needed someone who would never let me go."

He dragged her into his wet arms, holding her to him tightly as she cried, wishing to go forward in time again, if only to punish both of her parents for having done this to his queen.

But at the same time, he could no longer curse his fate or hers. What had happened to them both was the reason the spell had delivered him across time to her, his fated mate, his dark beauty, the one he had always been destined to love above all others.

CHAPTER TWENTY-ONE

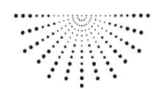

CHLOE wore the scrap of fabric with what she called the "divorce spell" on it pinned inside her wedding dress, right next to her heart. Fenris teased her about making it into a memento, but she didn't care. It had shot past her woman's dagger as her most valued treasure, because it more than any told the story of how much Fenris loved her. And at the wedding when she and Fenris drank a special non-alcoholic version of bridal ale she'd concocted from the same wolf-head shaped drinking vessel, she held her hand over the divorce spell, not caring that the pin pricked her skin. After this, she decided, she'd wear it inside her tunic, as a daily reminder. She'd never forget her Viking would never abandon her.

At that point the festivities had been going on for nearly a week. The trading boats had returned, and it was the rare day that everyone in the village was given leave by Fenris the Serious to put aside their work and celebrate. Also, hundreds of alpha chieftains and their contingents had come from far and wide to celebrate the wedding of their king. The wolves of their village were taking full advantage of the many feasts and all the new faces. It caused Uncle Olafr to joke that at least two or three she-wolves would have gone into heat by the time the festivities were over. At least she thought he was joking.

In any case, to her great relief, though the young wolves flirted madly, with one of the alpha chieftains even putting in a heat night claim for Aunt Bera's daughter, no one actually went into heat. And though the festivities went on for many days, it felt like Chloe blinked her eyes, and suddenly it was time for the wedding banquet. In her time, wolves married as any pregnant human would—as close as possible to the conception date, so as not to have a bride with a significant bump, and in one day with the usual wedding and reception to follow.

In this time, though, not only did they spend a week celebrating, but they also set up a small market so their many guests could trade and barter throughout the festivities. Instead of a receiving line, she and Fenris received many visitors in their longhouse over the week. While most weddings took place in the spring and summer in her time, most Norse wolf weddings took place as close to the fall harvest as possible, so as to ensure enough food for the festivities – there were even a few cases of wolf couples getting married after their pup was born if the conception happened right after the harvest times. And instead of a reception after the wedding, there was a wedding banquet before the ceremony.

Not coincidentally, every wolf but she and Fenris, was pretty drunk when they all spilled from their house to the meadow between the lake and the forest right before the moon was set to rise. Apparently they did not understand the meaning of solemn occasion, because Chloe could barely hear herself speak her vows above the hooting and hollering of the wolves of Norway, who all stood naked as the day they were born in a semi-circle around them.

But then, thankfully the moon rose, robbing all of the guests, except for Fenris and her, of their human speaking voices. Still, the wolves did manage to create quite a bit of ruckus as Fenris presented Chloe with a golden ring on the hilt of his sword. They howled to the sky, even more so, when Chloe put a gold band for Fenris on *The King Maker* sword and pushed the hilt back towards him to take.

But the biggest howls of all came when they kissed much longer than necessary under the light of the full moon, which hung large and low in the sky that night.

When they finally broke off the kiss, Fenris raised his sword in the air and pointed it toward the forest. It was Norse wolf tradition that the groom lead the pack on a hunt to fell a deer, while the bride went back to their home to prepare their bed with *goldgubbers*, palm-sized gold plates with wolves imprinted on them.

"Make quick work of the bed, beauty," Fenris said inside her mind as he ran toward the forest with the other wolves at his heels. "As I will make quick work of this deer, so I might have the pleasure between your legs that much sooner."

"I'll get it decorated as fast as I can, considering I'm carrying a bowling ball around."

"I know not what you mean by 'bowling ball,'" he answered, somewhat predictably.

"Yeah, yeah, yeah," she said, heading back to the village. "I'm going now."

She just hoped she was at least able to make it back to the longhouse before Fenris did. He was nothing if not quick, and as Rafe might have said, "Dude knows how to hunt."

She smiled thinking of Rafe and Colorado. They were now like a memory that was good until it got bad, but then got good again, because she was now so happy. Rafe would eventually find another she-wolf, hopefully one who pleased him in every way as Fenris said often of her. And eventually his anger would fade, and he'd see their split, though dramatic and humiliating, was for the best.

Her thoughts were abruptly cut short by a low growl and the

sudden stench of a wolf who had not taken his Saturday bath in a very long time.

She froze in her tracks when she saw a large red wolf, standing halfway between her and the door of the king's longhouse.

Fenris had assured her all wolves were trained to be in control of themselves while in wolf form and she had seen for herself over the course of her seven months in the village how much more civilized they were in wolf form than people from her own time.

But she could tell just by looking at this wolf that he wasn't civilized. Though, he wasn't frothing at mouth, his gray eyes looked crazed.

She took two steps back and the wolf took as many steps towards her, crouching low.

"Fenris?" she said, calling his name out loud, because she didn't quite know what to do.

Then the wolf charged her. She cried out and ran, hoping to God there wasn't a distance limitation on telepathy as she yelled, "Fenris! Fenris! One of the wolves is after me, it's trying to—"

A growl pierced the air beside her, right before the stinky red thing threw itself at her back, pitching her forward. She caught herself on her wrists, keeping her belly from hitting the ground. She had to protect the baby, she thought. But she also had to protect herself.

"Chloe? Chloe?" she heard the Viking ask frantically inside her head. "By Fenrir, answer me!"

The wolf lunged at her, burying its sharp teeth in her side, as if its sole intent was to tear the baby out of her womb. Red-hot pain ripped through her side, and she nearly passed out when he opened his jaw wide and sank his long, hot teeth into her again.

She screamed partly out of pain, but mostly out of terror.

But then she remembered the woman's dagger, the one she

had worn, only to tease Fenris about always nagging her to wear her dagger.

"Tis your wedding gift," she had said in her joking speech after recounting for their guests how often they'd gone back and forth about this.

But now she ripped it from the looped belt from which it hung, and she didn't know where the strength came from, but she, Chloe Adams, who was too squeamish to even wring a chicken's neck, stabbed the crazed wolf in his gray eye.

It let go of her side with a screech of pain. And Chloe followed it, her mind pitch-black with rage over what he had done to her and her baby. She stabbed it over and over again, in the heart, in the other eye, in the stomach, until it let out one last hideous yelp and morphed back into a human form, a young man with unwashed red hair, who she would bet money was Fenris' cousin.

And only then did she feel the cramping in her pelvis and the dampness. Between her skirts.

"No, no, no, not now," she cried in realization.

Her water had broken.

❇

*F*enris was closing in on a deer he could smell about half an acre away when Chloe pushed into his mind, "Fenris! Fenris! One of the wolves is after me, it's trying to—"

And his heart went cold when she cut off mid-sentence.

"Chloe? Chloe?" he asked, already turning around and running the other way, much to the surprise of the wolves he was leading in the hunt. "By Fenrir, answer me!"

The other wolves did not understand what was going on, but nonetheless, they followed him as a pack. Then they heard her scream. And this time it was not in ecstasy as his family had teased her for before. It was a scream of pain.

Fenris ran. Faster than he had ever run without shifting into a wolf as he did so. He had missed shifting over the course of the last seven moons, but never as much as he did now when he was confined to this human body while the woman he loved above all others screamed in the distance.

The other wolves also became compelled by the scream and they left him behind. He hoped to Fenrir they got to her in time, before... no he couldn't finish the thought. It made his vision go red at the edges.

"Chloe? Speak to me. Let me know you are unharmed, beauty."

Again, no answer.

And as he ran down the village's main thoroughfare toward her scent, he could now smell the thickness of her blood in the air as well as the acrid stench of his cousin.

He rounded the corner toward his longhouse and spied his cousin's human body lying in the distance, eyeless with angry stab wounds in his heart, stomach, and the side of his head. He would find out later his queen killed the large wolf, with nothing but her will to live and her tiny woman's dagger. And that would make what happened soon after much harder for him to bear.

But at that moment, his eyes searched around for her, until he realized she must be inside the large gathering of wolves.

He shoved through the pack and found his aunt and a few of his family pack members licking the deep wound in her side, cleaning it the only way they knew how in their present form. But even they he shoved aside to get to his bride.

She looked up at him with tears of pain and frustration in her eyes. "Fenris, my water broke. And I'm having contractions. The baby is coming. But it's too soon. We're going to lose him."

He raised her hand, which was still covered in his cousin's wolf blood, to his lips. "Nay, this I will not allow."

She breathed hard through the pain of her cramping. "I'm so sorry. I wanted us to be a family so badly."

"I will not allow it, beauty." He kissed her hand again. "You said if a baby is born in seven full moons in your time, your magic people might save it."

She caught his meaning and began shaking her head even before he could fully explain it. "No, no! You can't send me back."

He reached into her wedding dress. "I must, beauty. Your wound is deep and your waters have already broken. You cannot shift to heal, and we have no human medicine in the village. There is no other way."

She tried to slap away his hand, but he managed to unpin the spell. And this was when she began to sob. "No, I don't want to leave you. And you said you wouldn't abandon me."

His heart tore at the sight of her tears and he once again took her hand, holding it to his chest fiercely. "And I will hold fast my promise. I will find a way back to you, beauty."

"How?" she asked, shaking her head. She then clenched her teeth when another contraction overtook her. They were coming fast now. He could not linger here with her.

"I do not yet know. But I will. I promise you this on my life. I will be your mate and a father to our pup, and we will be as one again."

He kissed her sweet lips and then her forehead, which was damp with sweat despite the bitter chill of night.

Then before she could protest again, he yelled out to the other wolves to back away from her body, which they did.

With one last longing look toward the woman who had shown him a happiness he had never thought to know, he spoke the words to send her back to her own place and time.

"No, Fenris," she screamed, but it was too late. The black tunnel opened up just beyond her and sucked her into it as if she were but a pebble on the ground.

CHAPTER TWENTY-TWO

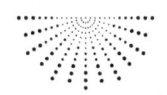

COLD and pain. Pain and cold. That was all Chloe knew at first when she landed outside the portal on Wolf Mountain. First she just lay there in the snow, her stomach cramping, wondering why no one had come to get her yet.

Then she heard growling, and two black wolves, one large, one small, appeared less than a meter away. And that's when she remembered it was still a full moon night, and moreover, she was back in her time, where shifter's "got wolf" whenever the full moon rose in the sky.

Not again, she thought, reaching for her woman's dagger, only to realize she must have dropped it after killing the last wolf.

She resorted to throwing rocks at the two black wolves, hoping it would be enough to stave them off for a while before the sun rose.

It wasn't. Chloe's aim wasn't great and neither was the strength she put behind it. The larger wolf barely flinched as it continued to advance. And soon it was so close, all Chloe could do was squeeze her eyes shut and shield her throat, as it leapt at her, jaw open wide.

But then she heard a big thump. When she opened her eyes, the dawn's earliest light had broken across the sky and the Colorado king lay there in human form, naked as a jaybird, with his equally naked wife lying just a few meters beyond.

"Goddamit, not you again," the king declared when he saw her lying there in the snow.

But the queen, the still very pretty Latina with the same light brown eyes as Rafe, framed by a polished bob, rushed over and fell to her knees beside Chloe. "She's hurt. Really hurt, and in labor, I think." The queen lifted her skirts up. "Oh my God, Dale, I can see the head crowning."

And then Chloe passed out.

But apparently the alpha couple decided against letting her and her baby bleed to death in the snow. When she woke, she did so in the clinic's hospital bed, dressed in a fresh hospital gown, with only the bandages on her side and the fact that she was wearing some sort of hospital diaper the only evidence she had been attacked by a wolf and forced into early labor.

"Where's the baby?" she asked Doc Fischer when he came strolling in. "Did he make it?"

"Oh, he made it, all right," Doc Fischer answered with an uncharacteristic smile. "Queen Lacey ended up delivering him right there on the mountain. The king had to run and get a Swiss Army knife out of his pants to cut the umbilical cord. But from what they told me, your pup shifted almost before King Dale could get the job done. Like he knew if he had any chance of survival, he had to let his wolf half have him as soon as possible. They showed up at my door with you passed out, looking like a Renaissance Fair murder victim, and this dark red wolf puppy in their arms. Let me tell you, my old eyes didn't know what to think."

He chuckled, like the drama of her life was some kind of campfire story. Then as if to confirm her assessment, he said, "Boyo, I'll be telling your story at parties for years to come."

"Can I see him?"

"Sure! He morphed back into his human form with fully developed everything a couple of hours ago. Hell of a kid, I tell ya. That Viking of yours must have some strong genes."

The only thing that kept her from dissolving into tears at that point was her fierce need to see her son and assure for herself he was all right.

And he was. The nurse brought him in from the other room, and he was nothing less than perfect. A light brown butterball of a baby with a head full of red curls, and deep brown eyes that were very clearly her own.

"Hello," she said, happier than she'd ever been to meet anyone.

He reflexively grabbed her finger, and squinted against the clinic's bright light.

At that moment, Chloe knew love at first sight, and she wondered why she had ever had the audacity to fear love. For one look into her son's bright eyes, and it was explained that what had happened between her parents, what had subsequently happened to her, was due to the absence of love, not a surplus of it.

Real love could never be toxic. Real love didn't lead you to leave your pup at the side of the road in order to be with your mate. No, real love, she realized, had been Fenris sending her back in time if it meant both she and the baby might live. And real love would be what brought them back together.

"We'll all be a family again," she whispered to the baby, kissing his dewy soft forehead. "I promise you."

CHAPTER TWENTY-THREE

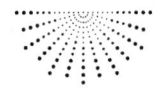

Chloe had promised their baby they would be reunited with his father, and she'd meant it. She had every faith Fenris would keep his promise and return to Colorado for them.

Only, he didn't. One full month—which Chloe was still counting in full moons—passed. Fenris Junior, or F.J., as she had taken to calling him, continued to thrive, breast-feeding like a maniac and charming his mother at every turn just by being alive.

But unlike when she went into mating frenzy with Fenris, this time she had some help with tackling this significant milestone. Much to Chloe's surprise, on her fourth day back, the alpha queen showed up at the clinic to drive F.J. and her to Chloe's old house, which she'd taken the liberty of dusting and converting the guest bedroom into a nursery.

"What about...?" Chloe asked, when she stepped into the room, which now had a crib and changing table on the wall opposite of the small guest bed.

"I'll handle him," Lacey answered, stringing her arm around Chloe's shoulders.

The Colorado queen appeared on her doorstep every day that

first month, ostensibly to bring her extra food, but really to hold F.J. for an hour or two while Chloe took care of certain practicalities like showering and packing up the house.

They had a few unspoken rules. They didn't talk about the king and queen almost tearing her apart in wolf-form on the mountain, and they didn't talk about Rafe, who from what Chloe could glean, still hadn't returned from his Alaska trip. She wondered briefly if he would eventually become engaged to the king's oldest daughter, Janelle, who was incredibly sweet, and who reminded Chloe of Rafe's mother. But she didn't dare ask.

Instead she rushed to get everything she needed to square away her modern life while she waited for Fenris. She turned off all the utilities, canceled all of her credit cards, closed her bank account, and either sold or liquidated all of her assets, so she'd have cash on hand until Fenris returned.

But then another full moon passed, and she realized unless she wanted to spend Christmas in an unheated house, she might need to apply a little of her DIY spirit to reuniting her family.

The day after the November full moon, she asked Rafe's mother if she could babysit F. J. for the whole day. The queen quickly agreed, telling her to bring F.J. and all the supplies by in the morning.

Chloe thought it would be a simple hand off at the door. But after Lacey took the baby from her, she insisted Chloe come into the living room for a bit, where, to her surprise, they found the alpha king waiting.

"Is that little F.J.?" he boomed, rising off the couch to meet them at the living room's arched entrance. "I've been missing you, little guy. Come here."

"Shhhh! You're going to scare him," the queen said, swatting at his arm.

"What, this little guy isn't scared of nothing, are you?" Without so much as a by your leave, he plucked F.J. out of his wife's arms and settled him into the cradle of his own. "You should've seen him on that mountain, Clo. He shifted so quick. Told mean old death, 'Hey, man, I'm not having none of that!' Never seen anything like it. This pup right here's going places."

Chloe could only look at the queen confused.

"I know he was angry at you before because of what happened with Rafe. But after the incident on the mountain, what we almost did..." The queen blushed. "He felt very badly about that. He's actually the one who bottle-fed F.J. while he was still shifted and healing. The truth is he's been begging me to get you to let him babysit for weeks. I doubt I'll actually get much time with him today."

"No, you will not," the king assured her. "Me and F.J. here have got big plans. First a manly man's breakfast. Then we've got that city council meeting. Then we're coming home and watching the Broncos game. Isn't that right? Isn't that right?"

He rubbed his index finger on F.J.'s belly and the baby belched out a happy gurgle.

"Dale, you are not going to take a baby to the city council meeting."

"Watch me," the king answered. "And if any of them wolves try to give me guff about it, I want you to poop on them. Okay, little man?"

As if in answer, F.J. let out a happy screeching sound that could easily be taken as an affirmative.

"Yeah, that's right. This pup gets it. He really does." He then turned to Chloe and held out his hand. "Hey can I borrow that doo-hickey you've got on? Probably come in handy at the meeting."

Completely baffled by this sudden turn of events, Chloe unstrapped the Baby Bjorn from around her body and placed it in his outstretched hand. "Um, okay...just call if you need anything, I guess."

"We won't," Rafe's father said as he walked out of the room, singing "Are You Ready for Some Football?" and bouncing F.J. in the air.

❄

*P*rofessor Henley was even more enthusiastic to see her than the Colorado king had been to see F.J. He met her outside of Sturm Hall, all but bouncing from foot to foot with excitement.

"Come, come!" he said without preamble. He grabbed her hand and led her into the building. "You won't believe what I've found."

Professor Henley led her into a cluttered office with a least ten standing pillars of dusty textbooks stacked as high as her head and two walls worth of bookshelves stuffed with texts of varying sizes. His only guest chair was covered in what looked like a pile of student papers, which he recklessly pushed aside, telling her to "Sit! Sit!" as they scattered on the floor.

She sat. "So were you able to find anything about the fated mates spell?" she asked.

"In a word: no," he answered, taking a seat of his own behind his desk. "After I got your call, I started searching for anything that would lead me to that original spell. But as you know, werewolves, due to wanting to keep our existence secret from humans, have an unfortunately rather oral history—I believe you said your friend in Alaska was working on getting more of it down on paper for her graduate study, if I'm remembering correctly. That's good work she's doing. It's shameful how little we wolves know about our own history."

As much as Chloe admired Alisha for the same reasons as Professor Henley, she was way more concerned with the fact that he hadn't found out anything new about the fated mates spell. "So why were you so happy when you met me outside if you didn't find anything?"

He grinned. "I didn't say I didn't find anything. I said I didn't find anything out about the fated mates spell. Your Fenris's aunt and her peers did a good job of keeping that one under wraps. If there was ever another case of a sorceress writing it down as she did for your wolf, they were very good about making sure it didn't fall into the wrong hands. Also, charcoal on linen has an expiration date, so there's no way even the most careful archaeologist would have found it.

However, after the fated mates spell turned out to be a dead end, I decided to start looking for any mentions of the Fenris I could find. That would be a little harder, and I thought I might have to travel to your friend's university in Alaska since they have a much bigger collection than we do. And just in case, I wanted to get as much information about the only thing we have of your Viking in this time. His sword. But when I looked it up again, I found a detail I hadn't noticed before."

He turned the computer monitor on his desk around to show her a blown up picture of what she immediately recognized as Fenris's sword set on a sheet of red velvet for it's formal museum photograph. "I don't understand. What's so great about finding Fenris's sword—"

But then she blinked, seeing what the Professor had. Seeing what hadn't been on the sword when she knew Fenris. "Oh, my God, there are words. Words on the sword!"

"I haven't been able to translate the runes fully yet, but I think they say—"

"Come back to me my fated one, so we may once again be as one," she supplied. Then she said the words again in Old Norse.

"Your Old Norse is very good," the professor said. He pulled out his smart phone and set it to record. "Could you repeat that? When's the next time I'll have a chance to hear Old Norse from an almost native speaker?"

She dutifully repeated the words three more times into the recorder, before asking,

"Do you think the words are some kind of spell or a clue about how to find the spell we need?"

As if in answer, her phone started ringing. Under any other circumstance, she would have let it go to voicemail, but she saw from the caller ID it was Rafe's mother.

"Hi," she answered the phone. "Is F.J. okay?"

"Oh, he's fine," the queen answered, her voice perfectly pleasant. "But the gate just flashed and my husband told me to call you…"

"Tell me, please tell me you did not bring that goddamn Viking forward in time again," he yelled in the background.

"Dale, watch your language around the baby!" she shouted back. Then her voice returned to its usual queenly dulcet when she asked Chloe. "So you wouldn't happen to know anything about that flash would you?"

CHAPTER TWENTY-FOUR

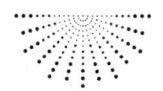

CHLOE had never driven so fast in her life. She nearly skidded a few times, as she came up the curvy mountain road to get back to Wolf Springs. But it still wasn't fast enough. When she got there, she found her Viking once again passed out in the clinic, sleeping off a tranq. But this time he didn't look nearly as vital as the first time he'd come. His body was still strong and rippling with hard muscle. But underneath the beard he'd once again grown, his cheekbones looked almost sunken in. And there were dark circles under his eyes.

"For a king, this guy doesn't have a hell of a lot of diplomacy. He not only put a dagger to the king's throat, but the poor queen had to shoot him with the tranq gun. Again."

"I'm sure he wasn't planning to really hurt the king. He just wanted the king to take him to me. If he was really looking to kill, he would have brought out his silver-plated sword."

Both Doc Fischer and the king gave her a sour look. "Uh-huh," said Doc Fischer. "Well, it's a good thing we got him back down the mountain. He's severely dehydrated, and from what I can tell, malnourished. It's like he's been on some kind of hunger strike or something. We hooked him up to an IV, though, so you two should be good to…do whatever you plan to do in a couple of days."

She took the Viking's IV-less hand before asking the king, "Where's F.J.?"

"The wife and I left him with Doc here while we went up the mountain and now the queen has him back at the house. By the way, if you want F.J. to spend the night with us, that's A-okay with us. We've got a travel pack-and-play in the attic. And you left enough breast milk to feed a baby wolf army."

She stroked the side of the Viking's face. "I might take you up on that."

"Might or definitely?" the king asked after the doctor left the room. "Because F.J. was excited about helping me make my famous pancakes in the morning. Maybe you and the Viking can stop by and have breakfast. But tell him to leave the dagger at your place."

She laughed. "I will. Thank you. Thank you for everything."

Dale started to turn to leave, but she had one more thing she had to say, since who knew if they'd ever have a chance to talk alone like this again. "And King Nightwolf, I just want to say again that I'm so sorry I hurt your son, and even more sorry I won't get to have you as a father-in-law. Whoever Rafe mates with is going to be a very lucky she-wolf."

The king waved a dismissive hand. "Ah, forget about what happened with Rafe. I've never doubted you were a great gal. I just had a feeling from the beginning that you and him weren't meant to be. My grandma had a little of the future reckoning in her. Maybe I inherited it from her."

"Maybe."

"But don't bother yourself too much about Rafe. He'll get over it. Eventually. Maybe. Okay, probably not. He's pretty bitter. But you got bigger things than him to worry about right now. We'll talk some more when you pick up little wolf for breakfast."

He saluted her and walked out.

Just then, the Viking began to stir. At first he looked around confused, his tangled red hair whipping across his face as his hand automatically went for the sword at his back. But then he saw her, and smiled. The most beautiful smile she had ever seen. It reached all the way into his eyes and seemed to emanate from his very soul.

"Beauty," he said. And he pulled her onto the bed with him, hugging her tight and strong. "Beauty."

She would find out later that after his aunt shifted back into human form, she told him there was a reunion spell that would deliver him again to his fated mate, but that it was almost impossible to cast, because it was necessary for both mates to say the words at the same time. Only after a full moon's worth of the most explosive grief of his life, because it looked like he would never make it back to his mate, did he remember what she told him about seeing his sword on the "internet." So he had the spell engraved in the sword, and from that moment forward, he ensconced himself in his bed closet, saying the words over and over again, barely pausing to eat or drink and only sleeping when it forcibly overtook him. For the rest of his life, his family would teasingly refer to him as Fenris the Chanting, for his actions over the weeks it took before the black tunnel opened and brought him back to her.

And he wouldn't care.

"It is you," he said bringing her hands to his chest with tears in his eyes. "The pup?" he asked, obviously fearing the worst because he wasn't present.

"Oh, he's good. He's great," she assured, tears also brimming in her eyes. "The Colorado king and queen are babysitting him tonight, and we're scheduled to see him first thing in the morning. He's, like, besties with the king now. It's kind of weird."

From the confused look on his face, he obviously didn't understand much of anything she said past, "He's great." But eventually his smile returned and he said, "Then it is us."

And this time tears spilled as she nodded. "Yes, it's us."

"We are not able to go to our son until the morn."

He continued to stroke her face, his own full of fondness. "And your medicine man has made it so your wounds have fully healed."

"Yes, I got the stitches out a few weeks ago, and I'm healed up pretty nicely."

"You are fully healed even though three full moons have yet to past?

"Yes, but what does that have to do with anything—"

Without further ado, he flipped her onto her back and was soon reminding her of when she told him in her time, she-wolves weren't allowed to have sex again until three full moons had passed after the birth of their pup.

She did think to protest. It had only been two months. And they were in a hospital bed with him attached to an IV. But then he yanked the IV needle out of his hand, and bit into her breast, just hard enough to get her attention. And just like that, she felt herself creaming down below as the scent of her arousal rose up in the air and any reservations about having sex with her fated mate flew out of her head.

His own scent, all forest, and longhouse, and burning fires filled her nose as he covered her with his body, before driving himself into her. He then lowered his head to her shoulder and began moving on top of her, almost frantic with his thrusts, as if he were trying to bury himself inside of her, so that they may never be parted again.

And maybe he achieved his aim. A climax rose quickly within her and she exploded just as he began to groan his release. For a glorious few moments, they were joined as one, locked together in both space and time in a starburst of pleasure beyond anything either of them had ever known.

And as she came down from the stars, breathing hard, she knew this time they would get it right. They were fated mates, and from this moment on, they would be together always.

EPILOGUE

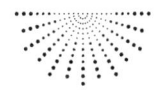

THIS past February, a Viking alpha king showed up in the shifter town of Wolf Springs and claimed the she-wolf then engaged to Colorado's alpha prince, as his fated mate. She reportedly did not want to honor the claim and still planned to mate with the alpha prince as soon as she went into heat. But then she unexpectedly went into heat on the night of a full moon, which kept her in human form. For reasons, still not quite understood, the Viking alpha king also didn't shift and he somehow found his way to her.

By sunrise the next morning, the entire town knew by the sounds coming from the house that the alpha prince's fiancée was now mated to another. The alpha prince left town, and once the she-wolf came out of a mating frenzy, she also attempted to leave town and the Viking behind. No one is quite sure where she was planning to go, but the sheriff caught her and dragged her back for a reason that still hasn't been fully explained—this historian is also fairly sure it wasn't legal. The Viking was permitted to visit her, but when they came back to the clinic's cage to fetch him, both the Viking king and the she-wolf had disappeared.

This was thought to be the end of it, but then seven months later, the she-wolf came back through the portal, wounded and in labor with a son, who was delivered by the Colorado alpha king and his queen them-

selves. The woman stayed on for two months, waiting to be reunited with her mate. Then she left her newborn with the royals in order to visit one Professor Henley. It is not known what they talked about, as the professor refuses to meet with me, but according to other sources, during their visit a flash was seen in Wolf Springs and reportedly the Viking came back through the gate.

He spent a mere forty-eight hours in Wolf Springs. During which he recovered from an undisclosed illness and met his son for the first time. An eyewitness, who happened to be in the room at the time, said it was a very touching scene to see the Viking meet his son for the first time.

Then reportedly Chloe Adams drove into Denver to pick up two period costumes, one for an adult and one for an infant, which she paid for in cash. Shortly after that, all three family members disappeared, never to be seen or heard from again.

And this report would be a whole lot longer if Rafe Nightwolf wasn't such a selfish, entitled, jerky douchebag!!!!!!!

Alisha Ataneq punched this last sentence in with particular force, since her recent visit to Wolf Springs had been such a bust. Her big mistake had been waiting until the end of the fall semester to make it. By that time, Rafe Nightwolf had finally returned to Wolf Springs and accepted the alpha king title, which he'd gotten ostensibly because his father was ready to retire, but more so, in Alisha's opinion, because he was a spoiled brat and his overly indulgent parents wanted to give him some kind of consolation prize for losing his fiancée to a time-traveling Viking.

But as a result, not many people had been willing talk to her about what had really happened to Chloe Adams.

A knock on her open door interrupted her thoughts and she looked up to see Matt, one of the other wolf post-docs at the University of Alaska-Juneau, standing at the entrance to her office. He was one of the few other wolves she knew her age who hadn't gone into heat yet, and she halfway suspected that, ensconced among humans as they were, they were probably both destined to either go unmated for life or mate with each other.

But if she did go into heat, she wouldn't mind doing so with Matt. He was cute in a string-bean nerd sort of way, and at least he was also in the humanities. She already knew her mom wouldn't approve though. Since Alisha was the second daughter of the Alaska alpha king, her mom preferred she marry some ridiculous but rich jerk like Rafe Nightwolf, not a fellow academic like herself. However, her mother's snobbery only made a guy like Matt that much more attractive to her.

"You busy?" he asked.

She threw him a friendly smile. "I can make myself un-busy. What's up?"

He edged himself into one of her guest chairs. "Well, I have some good news and some bad news and some possibly good news."

Before she could ask to hear the bad news first he said. "The good news is I think I might have found those diaries you asked me to keep a look out for."

Ever since she had all but abandoned her research on she-wolves in post-colonial Alaska, she had started putting most of her time and energy into finding out as much about the Vikings as she possibly could. She'd asked Matt, who did his work study in the wolf wing, a secret section of the library built under the cloak of night back in 1972, when the university was first established, to look for a few things for her, including the diaries of an Arab diplomat named Ibn Fadlan.

According to the annals of history, he had traveled around Norway, meeting many Vikings and journaling his experiences. But many of those manuscript pages had now "disappeared." As a Lupine History post-doc, she knew whenever a set of ancient records were found with a few missing pieces, that usually meant the wolves had gotten to them. The North American Lupine Council was near fanatical about keeping evidence of their existence out of the human purview, and very few universities even dared to keep a secret wolf collection. When they did, it was usually in fairly libertarian places like Alaska, South Dakota, and New Hampshire, states that liked their freedoms and weren't as scared of the North American Lupine Council as others.

"You found them," she said, leaning forward.

"I think so. Or at least a few manuscript pages that one of our wolves smuggled out of the secret collection at the University of Baghdad back in the nineties before the first Gulf war. My Arabic isn't that great, but I scanned it and put it through a translator and this passage caught my eye. If the translation program is working right, he talks about coming upon the village of King Fenris the Serious, which he finds puzzling, because the king is quite jovial. He is only received because the villagers think their queen, who he describes as 'a beauty, dark of skin,' might be interested in talking with him, because he also has darker skin. She speaks Old Norse, but in a dialect that is often hard for him to understand, and she won't tell him where she came from. And she is said to have three children, but he only meets two of them, a boy and a younger girl. But he says she also has a rather large wolf puppy, who stays crouched at the queen's feet and seems to be afraid of humans. The king and queen, who he describes as 'happy with each other in every way' receive him for three nights. But then the queen tells him that though she's enjoyed his company, it is best he move on before the next full moon. She tells him it is very important he and the Vikings he is with sail in a different direction than they originally planned, saying something to the effect of though they themselves are tame, she cannot be so sure about village to the north of them that calls no man king. They take her advice, but later on, one of the Vikings manning the ship Ibn is on says he suspects the foreign queen, the king, and their entire village are creatures of legend, ones who transform from human to animal in the light of the full moon."

Alisha's eyes widened and she took the translated pages from him. "That's her. I'm sure of it. I'm getting closer. How could there possibly be any bad news?"

"I was hoping you'd see it that way." He grimaced. "The bad news is the funding for your fellowship here has just been pulled and as of next semester, you'll no longer be employed by the University of Alaska."

"What!?"

He raised his hands. "The only reason I'm here telling you this is because I thought it should come from a friend as opposed to the head of the department, who's still pissed at you for pissing off the new king of Colorado.

Her eyes narrowed. "Tell me this sudden defunding doesn't have anything to do with Rafe Nightwolf."

Matt lifted his shoulders up and down. "What did you expect, Chloe? His family is one of the richest wolf dynasties in the United States. He has a seat on the council and the Nightwolf trust gives millions of dollars to the wolf residency program so shifters can attend state colleges all over the U.S. and enroll in wolf-based classes. He's not a guy you want to piss off. And you basically announced that you plan to write an entire book about the woman who left him for a Viking."

She shook her head. "How is no one understanding the impact Chloe Adams might have had on our own history? For all we know, she's influenced facets of our culture we don't even know about. How can you all stay so busy bowing and scraping to this jerk that you can be totally okay with not finding out what happened to her? Where's your curiosity?"

He gave her a sad smile. "Believe me, Alisha. I'm not happy about this situation either. It sometimes feels like the Council only funds us so they can keep us in check. But that brings me to the possibly good news. Now that you don't have a class load next semester, you can dedicate more time to solving the mystery of what happened to your friend."

She was still fuming, but she realized Matt was right. Rafe Nightwolf truly was an asshole for getting her fired, but that was about to blow up in his face. He thought he was shutting her down, but he had only fueled her determination to get to the bottom of this mystery. She would find out what happened to her friend, she vowed. And she wasn't going to let anyone, especially not Rafe Nightwolf, stop her.

❇

Thank you for reading the first book in the Alpha Kings series.

The next book in the series is WOLF AND PUNISHMENT—keep reading for the official preview.

Then comes Rafe's an Alisha's epic story, WOLF AND PREJUDICE! Make sure to check out all the books in the Viking Wolf saga:

ALPHA KINGS
Her Viking Wolf
Wolf and Punishment
Wolf and Prejudice
Wolf and Soul
Her Viking Wolves

ALPHA FUTURE
Her Dragon Everlasting
NAGO: Her Forever Wolf
KNUD: Her Big Bad Wolf
RAFES: Her Fated Wolf
Her Dragon Captor
Her Dragon King
Get them all at theodorataylor.com

If you loved HER VIKING WOLF, you'll also love the Amazon Bestselling Scottish Wolves series. So do check out HER SCOTTISH WOLF and HER SCOTTISH KING.

And to find out about new books, sales, and giveaways, make sure to sign up for my newsletter: http://theodorataylor.com/sign-up/

Thank you again, so very much for reading HER VIKING WOLF!

And keep reading for a sneak peek at WOLF AND PUNISHMENT….

> *Reviews are not something that I typically do however…the things that happen as they grow up and become the couple they need to be had me flipping my Kindle pages as fast as I could read.*
> **—Happy Amazon Reviewer**

※

Return of the big, bad wolf ex!

Two shifters from opposite sides of the tracks.

Two hot nights neither of them can forget—until he shows back up in her life—bigger, badder, and way more powerful than the boy she remembers.

He used to be a down-and-out prince. Now he's a KING who will settle for nothing less than red, hot revenge against the princess who broke his heart.

And revenge is best served QUEEN.

❄

*M*eeting her was like taking a bullet. Point blank. Straight to the heart.

Mag had agreed to accompany his roommate, Rafe, to Assault, a club popular with the Denver University football team. It was Friday night and he was bored. He hadn't expected this decision to change the course of his life. But that was what happened when a girl called out Rafe's name behind them as they headed inside.

"Rafe? Is that you?"

Mag turned to see a tall, thin she-wolf in an emerald green dress waving at them. She had long, wavy hair, and her skin was the color of one of those complicated coffee-drinks Rafe always ordered at Starbucks. Espresso, two shots of milk, and a pair of wide-set eyes that shined with fondness for his friend. Mag didn't have to be told she'd known Rafe for a long time.

"Janelle? What are you doing here?" Rafe smiled in surprise and pulled her into his arms for a hug while Mag stared like an idiot. He had never seen anyone so beautiful… between the covers of a magazine or in real life. Her delicate features were put together in such a way it made him think of woodlands and magical beings. The word fairy princess came to mind, even though he could smell the wolf inside her.

"Oh, I was asked to help judge this Miss Teen Wolf beauty pageant thing down the street, and they gave me a room at the Hotel Lusso since I was the only judge who had to fly in for it." She pointed at a four-story stone hotel across the street with tall arched windows and a canopy over its swinging glass doors. A guy in a striped vest and shiny shoes stood out front. Not his kind of place, Mag could tell right away. That doorman would probably call the police if a guy like him so much as stepped up onto the hotel's sidewalk.

"Why didn't you call me?" Rafe was asking her now. "You know I'm at Denver University."

"Well, I'm only in town tonight and I didn't want to bother you. You've got your human work and your wolf work for school. Plus, you're on the football team—I didn't want to make you play host."

"It wouldn't have been a bother at all. I mean, I'm obviously not studying right now." He jerked his head towards the club doors.

Her eyes twinkled. "Obviously."

Mag was barely following the conversation at this point. Janelle and Rafe had been talking in a half hug position for approximately thirty seconds. And even though Mag knew Rafe would never betray his pretty little fiancée, Chloe, with another girl—Lord knew, he had plenty of chances—Mag had to force himself not to pull this unknown she-wolf out of his best friend's arms.

Down, boy, he told his wolf. This she-wolf, he could already tell, wasn't for him. She had "good girl" written all over her: good clothes, good manners, good family for sure if she knew Rafe well enough to call him when she hit town. Rafe was the Alpha Prince of Colorado and he'd never put on any airs about it—hell, he was engaged to a scholarship she-wolf and lived in a crappy three-bedroom off campus because that had been all his two best friends, Mag and Grady, could afford. However, Mag suspected when Rafe wasn't picking up friends and fiancées from the Island of Impoverished Toys, he kept company befitting a wolf who would one day rule over the Colorado state packs.

Mag looked down at his own clothes, a howling wolf t-shirt, jeans, a pair of scuffed up motorcycle boots, and a jacket doing a bad job of pretending to be leather—all purchased at Wal-Mart. The howling wolf t-shirt was supposed to be ironic: look, a were-wolf wearing a wolf on his chest! But standing next to Rafe in his designer jeans and Italian leather jacket, he felt ashamed for not having the money to dress that well, for not being the kind of guy a girl like this would ever look at.

But then she did look at him, her eyes blinking a little, as if the same bullet that hit him when she appeared had just slugged into her.

"Hi," she said, stepping away from Rafe and turning toward him. She smelled like expensive perfume, snow, and ice. "I'm sorry for not introducing myself sooner. I'm Janelle."

She held out her hand. And he took it, trying to play it off like he didn't feel another bullet go through his chest when his large hand closed over her smooth palm and long, delicate fingers.

"M-Mag. Maguyuk Lonewolf, but—but everybody calls me Mag."

He was stuttering. He was actually stuttering, this girl had him so shook.

"He's my roommate. We're on the football team together," Rafe said beside him.

"Oh!" Janelle gave Mag a pleasant smile. "How nice to meet you."

She said this with such rote kindness, he got the feeling she spoke the words a lot. He didn't care. He was more than willing to make small talk if it meant keeping her there. "Nice to meet you, too. You wanna come in with us? Our friend Grady's on the door tonight, so we don't have to wait in line."

Janelle hesitated, seeming to consider the invitation. He didn't blame her. She was tall, but at six-four with a fuck ton of muscle and a wolf that hovered close to the surface, Mag knew he was intimidating—especially compared to Rafe, who literally was a prince and acted like one, treating everyone with the courteous respect of a ruler born. He was like a walking Benetton ad, thanks to a pair of sharp cheekbones from his Native American dad, dreamy hazel eyes from his ma, and a whole head of matinee idol hair (seriously, every ink-black strand stayed in perfect place no matter what—Mag had no idea how the dude did it). Rafe looked like every girl's dream come true. While Mag looked exactly like what he was—a long-haired Inuit thug who'd gotten into Denver University on a football scholarship.

However, Janelle surprised him by saying, "Okay, sure. I'll come in."

"Ladies first," he said, stepping aside so she could walk ahead of them to the club's door.

When Grady saw she was with them, he didn't even bother to check her ID, just unlatched the rope and let them in with nods for Mag and Rafe.

"Hot." Grady signed, his eyebrows lifting up toward his hairline as he watched her walk into the club, where she'd look way out of place in her designer cocktail dress—like an intricately carved ring in a pan of fool's gold.

Mag wasn't nearly as good at ASL as Rafe, but he recognized the sign for "hot" well enough. It had been one of the first signs Mag asked the tank-sized blond to teach him, back in the early days of their friendship when Grady's impairment had been a novelty as opposed to just one of many character traits belonging to someone he now respected very much.

But that respect didn't keep his wolf from growling silently. Like Janelle was his territory and Grady had just stepped over the line.

Rafe shook his head and signed something complicated back to Grady, which Mag assumed meant "off-limits," since a few seconds after he was done, Rafe looked back at him and said, low enough that Janelle wouldn't hear... even with her wolf ears, "She's a close friend of my family's. Her dad's like an uncle to me. You can look, but don't touch."

Mag nodded, weirdly liking how Rafe was so adamant about no one getting fresh with his family friend. Yeah, it meant Mag wouldn't be able to act on those two bullets she fired his way, but it also meant no one else could either.

And despite having only just met Janelle, he found he liked the idea of no other wolf touching her. Liked it a lot.

※

"What are you doing here?"

It was the second time Janelle had been asked that question tonight, but this time the circumstances weren't nearly as pleasant. Kenny Lacer appeared in front of her like an unwelcome cold front on an otherwise lovely fall night, beer in one hand and a blonde with a butterfly tattoo on her chest practically hanging off his side.

Janelle struggled to keep the pleasant expression on her face. It was just her luck the Wyoming Beta was here. The Denver U. football team was one of the best in the division, mainly because it served as a feeder system for betas. The biggest, toughest wolves from across the land were sent there to not only play football, but also to hone the skills they'd need to serve as the first line of defense between a challenger to a state crown and the king the crown already belonged to.

Kenny, in particular, was a nasty piece of work: a cousin of the Wyoming royal family who'd done well in football and had agreed to be the alpha prince's beta in exchange for a pardon on charges stemming from his nearly beating to death a gay wolf who'd "looked at him the wrong way." Janelle wasn't surprised at all that the large, brown-haired wolf would patronize a club called Assault. She also had less than zero desire to talk to him, much less explain her presence at a human nightclub most she-wolf princesses wouldn't even know existed.

But he was the Wyoming prince's beta, so…"I was actually across the street judging a…" she glanced at the blonde—a human who wouldn't know werewolves were way more than a legend, "…small beauty pageant, when I saw Rafe coming in here with his friend." She pointed toward the bar where Rafe and Mag were getting drinks.

The blonde looked over to where Janelle was pointing. "Ooh, they're cute!" she chirped.

Kenny gave her a look that could have withered a flower on its stem, even if it was technically a weed like this girl, and handed her his beer. "Go stand over there and wait for me," he told her like she was a dog at his command.

But the blonde didn't seem to mind the order. "Okay, sure, I'll be right over there!"

After his human was gone, Kenny looked over his shoulder at Rafe and Mag, then back at her. "Not sure the Wyoming prince would approve of you being out with two guys."

Janelle held onto her pleasant expression, revealing nothing of what she was feeling inside, a skill that had been painstakingly drummed into her since birth.

"Rafe invited me here, and as you must know, my family and his are long time allies. I'm sure the Wyoming prince would understand how rude it would be if I turned down an invitation from a family friend—one happily pledged to another wolf whom I admire greatly."

Kenny chewed over her defense, like a sullen dog with an old bone. "Yeah, I've never seen Rafe with anyone but that Chloe chick, but..." Kenny looked Janelle up and down, like he was running a leer-based lie detector test over her body, "...that guy he's with, Mag—he hooks up with a lot of human chicks. I'm not comfortable with you hanging out with him, even if the Prince of Colorado is chaperoning."

And that was when the situation got really awkward. Was Kenny telling her she had to leave the club? Yes, she realized, he was, and his presumption made Janelle's cheeks burn with resentment. He shouldn't be ordering her around! She was a princess, not some weed of girl he'd just met at a bar.

However, she knew if she didn't do as Kenny said, he'd call the

Wyoming prince. Then his parents would call her parents, and she'd be made to fly to Wyoming to smooth things over. And that would mean days of having to act like the Wyoming prince didn't set her teeth on edge with his pompous attitude, his ridiculous sense of entitlement, and the way he acted like she was a trophy in his collection, one he owned body and soul. No, when she calculated the situation in her mind, defying Kenny wouldn't be worth the trouble she'd be in if she didn't do as he said.

"Okay," she said, keeping her voice cheery. "Just let me say goodbye to Rafe and I'll head back to my hotel."

There was no small amount of smug on Kenny's face as he nodded, "You do that."

Then he went back over to the blonde with the butterfly tattoo.

When Rafe and Mag came with the drinks, she greeted them with an apology. "I'm so sorry," she said before Rafe could hand her the glass of white wine she'd ordered. "I really misjudged how tired I was, and it's a bit loud in here... I think I should call it a night."

It wasn't even ten, the evening had barely gotten started, but Rafe, ever the gentleman, inclined his head with respectful acquiescence. "Of course, Janelle. I'll walk you back to your hotel."

"Oh no, there's no need! It's right across the street, and I'd hate to tear you away from your friend..." she glanced at the man beside him and that shiver went through her again. The one she'd never felt before.

That shiver had been what made her accept his invitation in the first place. The perennially good princess inside her had known it wasn't the best idea in the world, but something had pushed Janelle forward, wanting to know more about the wolf who had made her mind hiccup if only for a few seconds.

He had the name, brown-tinged skin and almond-shaped eyes of an Eskimo—he also smelled like an Alaskan Inuit wolf. However, there were two things that set him apart from most other Inuit wolves. The first was his eyes. Most Inuit wolves, even half-Inuit ones like her, had brown eyes, but his were a color too dark to be blue, too light to be gray. A mesmerizing silver that made her usually docile wolf raise up on it haunches and crane its neck. And even though the rest of his face was roughly planed with a hawkish nose, she hadn't been surprised when Kenny had crudely alluded to his high success rate with human women. No doubt those moon-colored eyes of his drew them in, just like they had drawn her.

The second thing that made her wonder if she wasn't smelling him wrong was he hadn't seemed to recognize her as one of the Alaska princesses when they met, which was... odd. Especially for someone who had been raised to know she would be recognized—recognized and judged by every Alaskan wolf wherever she went, not just because she was a princess, but because she was the first half-black princess the state had ever had, the product of the surprise mating between the state's Inuit king and her black mother, the former Princess of Detroit. The thought of someone from Alaska not automatically knowing who she was intrigued her. Intrigued her enough to accept an invitation from someone who clearly didn't walk in the same social circles as she and Rafe. But she could see now that accepting the invite had been a mistake.

She turned to the wolf and said, "Mag, I'm sorry for accepting your invitation only to bow out so suddenly. I'm usually not this rude. I'm just really tired."

The imposing football player, who from the brutal look of him, was probably also in line to be some prince's killer beta, maybe even Rafe's, studied her for a few beats before saying, "Nah, don't worry about it. Not a problem."

"Are you sure I can't walk you to your hotel?" Rafe asked again.

Janelle smiled. "The only thing I'm more sure of is how much I'd rather you stay here and enjoy the rest of your evening." She gathered her small Coach clutch to her chest and started to walk away with a wave before Rafe could argue any further. "Next time I'm in town I'll call you beforehand, and we'll schedule brunch, I promise."

"I'll hold you to that," Rafe called after her.

Janelle made a speedy retreat. As she walked to the door, she glanced at Kenny. He was sloppily kissing the blonde human, his beer still in hand and resting against her flat bottom. Apparently he was so confident she'd do as he ordered—like a good little princess—he didn't even bother to watch her go.

Sadly, his confidence hadn't been misplaced. Janelle rushed out of the club and across the street to the little boutique hotel where she was staying, like a child who was afraid of getting in trouble if she didn't mind.

But just as she passed the doorman who politely held one glass door open for her, she heard a voice behind her say, "Janelle."

She turned. It was the Inuit wolf from the club.

"Mag!" she said in surprise. He was so huge, he seemed to take up all the space beneath the canopy. But his silver eyes... they were kind and soft. Not dead and hateful like Kenny's.

"You all right?" he asked her in his deep, gentle voice. "I saw Kenny talking to you, then suddenly you had to go. Did he say something? He upset you?"

The way he asked the question made her wonder what he would do if she answered truthfully. Yes, Kenny did say something to me. Yes, he did upset me. But she was a first-born princess, which meant living a life made up of white lies.

She smiled politely. "No, he was just saying hello. We have friends in common. Like I said, I'm tired. But again, I'm sorry for leaving so early."

"Was it me?" he asked. "Did you cut out because of me? Cuz if you want to hang with Rafe, I can take the bus back to campus. They've got a shuttle, goes right through here."

"No! Please don't think you had anything to do with my leaving," she said, though technically he did, since his "hooking up with human chicks" was what prompted Kenny to demand she leave the club.

"Really, I'm tired," she said, even though she couldn't remember the last time she'd felt so awake. Talking to him, from the very first moment they'd clasped hands in greeting, had felt like waking up from her sleepy, well-ordered life on a roller coaster. And now that he was standing here in front of her hotel, sleep was the furthest thing from Janelle's mind. "But, um.... I was thinking of having a cup of hot chocolate before I went up to my room. Would you, ah… like to join me?"

❄

Rafe's friend, Janelle, seemed to be good at covering up her real feelings.

If she was nervous about sitting in a hotel bar with a wolf she just met, sipping hot chocolate, she didn't show it. He, on the other hand, was nervous as hell.

He couldn't believe he was here, sitting close enough to touch the most beautiful she-wolf he'd ever met. He could just imagine how the other guys on his team would laugh if they saw him now, sweating bullets over a virgin she-wolf after all the human girls he'd gone through during his three years at Denver U.

But here he was, a senior in college, Mr. Big Wolf on campus, and he could barely talk to this girl who'd invited him to sit down with her for a drink.

"So you play football with Rafe," she said after they'd received their steaming, fragrant mugs. She gave him another of her twinkling smiles, and he had to admit her game was tight. Like he could maybe see her hosting one of those morning talk shows his grandma loved so much.

"How do you like playing on a team together?" she asked. "It must be nice to share the field with your friend."

Mag shrugged. "He's a receiver and I'm a linebacker, so we don't really spend that much field time together."

She squinted a little, and a cute but confused look came over her face.

"We're on two opposite sides of the team. He's offense. I'm defense. The only time we ever play together is at practice and usually I'm trying to tackle him."

"Oh, I get it now." Her smile turned sheepish. "I suppose I should pay more attention when my father watches Seahawk games."

He inclined his head. "You from Alaska?"

That question seemed to throw her. "Yes, yes, I am," she answered.

He nodded. "Yeah, I should've guessed. You smell like Alaska and your dad roots for the Seahawks. Sounds like an Alaska wolf to me. I'm from Alaska, too."

"Oh, that's nice," she said, but she seemed tense now, as if she were bracing herself for something.

He'd never met an African-American wolf from Alaska before, and that made him even more curious about her. "Where do you live?"

"Wolf Lake," she answered carefully.

"You're from the kingdom town… oh…" He took a big interest in his napkin. So that confirmed it. She was out of his league. Way out of his league. Ever since the official King of Alaska got the state pack involved in the very lucrative oil business, only the richest wolves could afford to live in Wolf Lake, the kingdom town located in interior Alaska. From what he'd heard, you needed a plane just to get to the lake the town was named after. And then, if you didn't have a floater plane, you either had to row or walk across the large body of water, which took up the one side of the kingdom town that wasn't already surrounded by mountains.

"Yes," she said. "The lake should be freezing over soon, and we're already gearing up for the Arctic Wolf Games. Have you ever been?"

He peeled a strip of his napkin. "People from where I live aren't exactly invited to stuff like that."

"People from where you live," she repeated, then she realized out loud, "Oh, are you part of the Inu-Amaruq pack?"

Mag flexed his hands around the torn napkin. Inu-Amaruq—literally Bad Wolf. They were what used to be called a gypsy pack, back before Alaska officially joined the North American Lupine Union, and back before people, including the Inu-Amaruq themselves, had started taking offense at the word gypsy. Like their nomadic ancestors, they still followed the fish and game and built igloos for hunting—though only for hunting. When it came time to sleep, they hauled their asses back to their RVs like any sane hunter would if he had a choice.

Also, like their ancestors, they considered their own pack alpha their king, refusing to acknowledge the sovereignty of the state king or abide by the rules of the North American Lupine Council. All he knew of the kingdom town was it was hard to get to, even by their nomadic standards. He wouldn't have even been able to say for sure who the current state king was, though Rafe had mentioned when they first met that his father, the King of Colorado, and the Alaska king were best friends who'd played football together for Denver U.

When Rafe realized Mag knew absolutely nothing about his own state's royal family or politics, he'd dropped the subject, a renaissance wolf realizing he was speaking with someone who'd only known hunting and fishing and, if necessary, selling drugs and/or thieving, his entire life.

"Yeah, I'm from Inu-Amaruq," he said. "But we don't call it

that. We call it…" He told her the words, using the dialect of their tribe.

"What does it mean in English?"

"Freedom," he answered, refusing to be ashamed of where he was from, even if it sent her running for the hills, like it would have a lot of nice Alaska girls. "Technically Freedom Town, which I know sounds strange since we're always moving around. But we call ourselves a town because even if we're on the move, that don't mean we aren't a community, you know. And we call ourselves Freedom, because we make the rules. We're not living under some wolves in suits who probably don't even know how to hunt."

"Freedom Town," she repeated. She seemed to like the taste of the words in her mouth. "I've always wondered about Freedom Town."

This, Mag sensed, was true curiosity, and not her just trying to make conversation. "You got questions about my pack, you can ask 'em. Long as you're cool with me asking you about the kingdom town. You go first."

"Okay," she said with a grin. "First question: when you fly home from college, how do you find your pack if you're always traveling around?"

He chuckled. "We got satellite phones. I call my brother before I buy my ticket and he tells me where he thinks they're going to be when I come through. Then when I get to the airport closest to that place, he sends me the GPS coordinates for wherever they're at that day. It's kind of complicated. Too complicated. I'm going home with Rafe for winter break this year."

She took in what he'd just told her with a slow shake of her head. "Wow, I can't even imagine," she said. "Okay, it's your turn."

"Rafe told me the Colorado kingdom town has an invisible gate up in its mountains. Like a time gate, and he says wolves can travel through them if they have the right spell. I called him a liar, but Grady said Oklahoma has one, too. He said all the states do and that's how the werewolves know where to establish their kingdom towns. I think they're pulling my chain, but since you're from the Alaska kingdom town…"

She chuckled a little. "No, actually it's absolutely true. It's the —I mean, I hear it's the royal family's job to greet any visitors who come through. It's only gone off twice since I've been living in Wolf Lake. Both times it was she-wolves who'd traveled through time to meet their fated mates. But from what I hear, the Colorado gate gets a lot of activity. Apparently, Colorado wolves are way more attractive to the winds of destiny than Alaska wolves."

Mag laughed incredulously. "Yeah, I guess so. I still can barely believe they were telling me the truth, though. I better apologize for calling them ten different kinds of liars."

"Well, that would be the polite thing to do." She smiled at him again. "I wish I could tell you more about the gate. If my sister, Alisha, were here, she'd be able to tell you all sorts of stuff about it. She's in grad school to become a history professor, and I know she'd have so many questions about Freedom Town, too. Better than the ones I have—for instance, is it true your pack still get face tattoos whenever you kill someone?"

"Yeah, that's true," he said, his thoughts going to a dark place as his father's heavily tattooed face floated across his mind's eye.

"But you don't have any face tattoos," she said.

Her observation brought him back. "No, I don't."

She grinned. "So you're safe!"

"I've been called a lot of things before. Safe ain't one of them," he answered ruefully.

"I don't know," she said, taking another sip of her hot chocolate. "We're sitting here and you're from Bad Wolf and you're like this big, strong football player—you look like someone's beta— but I feel safe with you."

Her words warmed him, even more than the hot chocolate. "You are safe with me. You're Rafe's friend and you're nice, and you're... really beautiful." He admitted he'd been affected by her looks, even though he knew it was a thin line between admiring a girl and really creeping her out. "I'd never hurt you or let anyone else hurt you."

Her eyes softened and she looked at him for a long, long time before asking, "Is it also true what they say about male wolves from Bad Wolf? That you're not bound by Lupine Council law, so you guys can have sex with a she-wolf before she goes into heat?"

Mag considered lying to her. He hadn't thought about it much back when he'd been living in Alaska, when he'd slept with several willing she-wolves, not even aware such a law existed until he came to Colorado. Rafe had let him know about it during a wolf mixer, told Mag he could flirt with she-wolves in Colorado but if he wanted to go any further than that, he'd need to stick to human girls. It had seemed like a fucked up rule to him considering she-wolves couldn't contract sexually transmitted human diseases or get pregnant if they weren't in heat. Why not let the girl wolves have some fun before they mated up, too?

But now that Janelle-with her perfect hair, her sweet smile, and her twinkling eyes was asking him about sex in Freedom Town, the fact that he'd slept with several unheated females before landing at Denver U. made him feel less like a guy having a lot of fun before he settled down and more like a sleaze.

Still, he didn't want to lie to her. So he took a chance and told the bright and shiny girl sitting across from him the truth: "Yeah, that's true, too."

She set down her cup. "Have you ever slept with an unheated female?"

"Yeah, I have," he said, and he braced himself, wondering if she'd immediately get up and leave or keep making small talk until she finished the hot chocolate and could say goodnight without it being a thing.

But then she looked up at him and said, in a hushed voice, "Would you, um... would you sleep with me?"

Mag went completely still. He must have heard her wrong. Either that or he'd totally misunderstood what she was asking him.

"What?" His voice sounded hoarse even to his own ears.

She'd been cool as a cucumber before, but now he could feel the nervous energy coming off of her in waves. Her delicate fingers clenched and unclenched around her cocoa mug.

"Would you have sex with me? Would you take my virginity tonight?"

Then as if she'd just remembered her manners she added, "Please?"

Oh, my wolf!
What will Mag say?
Go to theodorataylor.com to finish reading
WOLF AND PUNISHMENT

ALSO BY THEODORA TAYLOR

ALPHA KINGS

Her Viking Wolf

Wolf and Punishment

Wolf and Prejudice

Wolf and Soul

Her Viking Wolves

ALPHA FUTURE

Her Dragon Everlasting

NAGO: Her Forever Wolf

KNUD: Her Big Bad Wolf

RAFES: Her Fated Wolf

Her Dragon Captor

Her Dragon King

ALIEN OVERLORDS (as Taylor Vaughn)

His to Claim

His to Steal

His to Keep

THE SCOTTISH WOLVES

Her Scottish Wolf

Her Scottish King

Her Scottish Hero

RUTHLESS MC

WAYLON: Angel and the Ruthless Reaper Book 1
WAYLON: Angel and the Ruthless Reaper Book 2
GRIFFIN: Red and the Big Bad Reaper
VENGEANCE: Snow and the Vengeful Reapers
HADES: Stephanie and the Merciless Reaper
HADES: Stephanie and the Ruthless Mogul

THE VERY BAD FAIRGOODS
His for Keeps
His Forbidden Bride
His to Own

RUTHLESS TYCOONS
Ruthless Scion
Ruthless Billionaire
Ruthless King
Ruthless Husband
Ruthless Captor

RUTHLESS TYCOONS: Broken and Ruthless
KEANE: Her Ruthless Ex
STONE: Her Ruthless Enforcer
RASHID: Her Ruthless Boss

RUTHLESS TRIAD
VICTOR: Her Ruthless Crush
VICTOR: Her Ruthless Owner
VICTOR: Her Ruthless Husband
HAN: Her Ruthless Mistake
PHANTOM: Her Ruthless Fiancé

RUTHLESS FAIRYTALES

Cynda and the City Doctor

Billie and the Russian Beast

Goldie and the Three Bears

Reina and the Heavy Metal Prince

(newsletter exclusive)

RUTHLESS BOSSES

His Pretend Baby

His Revenge Baby

His Enduring Love

His Everlasting Love

RUTHLESS BUSINESS

Her Ruthless Tycoon

Her Ruthless Cowboy

Her Ruthless Possessor

Her Ruthless Bully

RUTHLESS RUSSIANS

Her Russian Billionaire

Her Russian Surrender

Her Russian Beast

Her Russian Brute

HOT HARLEQUINS WITH HEART

Vegas Baby

Love's Gamble

ABOUT THE AUTHOR

Theodora Taylor writes hot books with heart. When not reading, writing, or reviewing, she enjoys spending time with her amazing family, going on date nights with her wonderful husband, and attending parties thrown by others. She LOVES to hear from readers. So….

Join TT's Patreon
https://www.patreon.com/theodorataylor

Follow TT on TikTok
https://www.tiktok.com/@theodorataylor100

Follow TT on Instagram
https://www.instagram.com/taylor.theodora/

Sign for up for TT's Newsletter
http://theodorataylor.com/sign-up/

Printed in Great Britain
by Amazon